IN AT THE DEEP END BY ALEXANDER GUNZ

Alexander Gunz is London-born and bred, having lived in the Edgware Road area all his adult life. He has two degrees (Philosophy, Politics & Economics, and English Literature). Alex works in finance by day. In his spare time, he is an avid reader (averaging at least 50 novels a year for the last two decades) and freelance restaurant reviewer. *In at the Deep End* is his first novel, written over the course of 2017, and published in 2019. Alex is currently working on a collection of short stories.

To my Father, who inspired in me a love of reading

IN AT THE DEEP END

by

ALEXANDER GUNZ

"But about feelings people really know nothing. We talk with indignation or enthusiasm; we talk about oppression, cruelty, crime, devotion, self-sacrifice, virtue, and we know nothing real beyond the words." (Joseph Conrad, 'An Outpost of Progress')

PROLOGUE

Outside, everything feels different. The air is colder, the night raw and sharp. Traffic streams past; past a young couple kissing, a dogwalker, a lady struggling with a handful of shopping bags, a confused old man, wobbling unsteadily along on his way. Vans are being unloaded, others reloaded. The sound of a distant siren makes me start. Maybe the others haven't noticed it. Or perhaps they have just pretended not to. My nerves are on edge. The food I ate earlier sits uncomfortably in my stomach. My mouth is dry and sticky. AJ and one of the other guys are walking ahead. He has his arm draped over AJ's shoulder, like they are mates. The two others who also came along are behind me on the street. I am in the middle, between the two groups, but feeling very alone. At least we are only a few minutes' away from AJ's house. When we get there, we will be warm again. And soon this whole thing will be over. I pause to retie one of my laces, look up and notice that the others have stopped, come to a standstill. But there is no zebra crossing here, nothing is blocking their way. They aren't lighting up cigarettes or checking their mobiles. Now I realise that they all seem to be arguing. But, why? We had everything agreed beforehand, before we left the last place. I also see clearly that their postures are urgent and intense. I move forward quickly to reach them. Then I see the sudden flash of something bright, silver and metallic. As I get closer, five paces, four, three, I have that terrible feeling, a sense of sinking, a looming realisation that things are definitely not right. There is the glint again. Time then halts. Or perhaps it flips, or maybe just does something funny, which I can't put a name to. I think of the cartoons I used to watch as a kid. The ones when the characters would chase each other in circles, then the bad guy would get to the edge of a cliff, his legs pedalling furiously as he realised there was nowhere to go but down. That's sort of what I feel like. We are now in a tight circle. I want to run, to be somewhere, anywhere, different, but I can't. I hope a passerby might notice us, but everyone I look at has their head down, probably pretending they have not seen us. Now I am falling. My legs want to do something, but my knees give way. Pain and confusion grip me. Thoughts crowd my brain. They come and go quickly. I want to catch them, cling to them, cling to anything as I tumble. But they fly away, as if they were butterflies. As I think of these beautiful insects, I see a kaleidoscope of colours whirling around me: the orange of street lights, now tumbling out of perspective; the red of buses, also losing focus. Then there is red everywhere, pooling around me. Other colours and pictures whizz before my eyes. I try to think of happier times: the greens I see remind me of football pitches, the blues of water and of swimming. Next come yellows, and I have images of the sun, large and fat in the sky. I want to be warm, but now I feel cold, so terribly cold, colder than I have ever felt before, shivering and shaking uncontrollably. All the colours are suddenly starting to blur. They speed up, then slow down, slow down, slow down. After that, there is nothing.

Part One: In

JOHN

John is twenty-two, fat and unhappy. His physical and mental states are probably not helped by the fact that he works at Perfect Pizza. Actually, he quite likes the greasy discs that masquerade as food. He doesn't object that much to the monotony of the job. The constant and seemingly unending assembly of the take-away boxes may be an almost Sisyphean task, but John has never been familiar with this, or indeed any other Greek myth. He is happy enough mopping the floor, filling the drinks cabinet and even clearing away the discarded remains; unwanted crusts, sorrowful chicken bones, the dregs of unfinished cans and other residue from late-night binges and drunken errors. He has yet to graduate to making pizzas. The biggest problem for John is that he is lonely. He barely knows anyone in London. And, he misses his Gran.

In what could be considered his more introspective moments, John sometimes feels that he got the short straw. It all began at a young age. He still carries the emotional scars inflicted by his two older brothers referring to him as "the accident." The name never made any sense to him in his early years. He was no more prone to falling over in the playground than his peers, not necessarily more unstable on his bicycle or liable to spill his drinks. His brothers were clever in their ribbing of John; it was almost never done in the presence of their parents. Not that Dan, his Dad, would have cared; all he ever talked about was the number of cars he had sold. Meanwhile, Sylvie, his Mum, had been mostly cowed into submission by years of domestic drudgery.

When he was somewhat older and thought to wonder why there was an eight-year age difference between himself and Philip, while Alan stood a further two years beyond that, only then did the nickname make sense to John. The more he thought about it, the more he realised that whatever skills his Mum and Dad may have had in parenting, they had apparently used them up on his siblings. Indeed, his brothers had made – somehow – what his parents called successes of themselves. Alan had gone to work in London, doing something important in a bank there. He had made lots of money, relocated to Hong Kong and was now married, with his own family and living in a big apartment. Apparently, it even had its own swimming pool. Not that John had ever visited, since an invitation never had been (and would likely never be) forthcoming. Whenever Alan did jet in to England it was rarely for any length of time and his general attitude towards John was one of disdain. Philip was even worse. He had gone into the same trade as his Dad. He was openly patronising and sneering towards John, making jibes such as "grow up and get yourself a proper job," or worse, "John, you're such a failure."

Much of it, John feels, as he stands there folding and folding again yet more pizza boxes, isn't even his own fault. Whereas Alan and Philip had both done well enough, at school, John had struggled, despite his best efforts. His siblings may not have excelled academically, but a combination of sporting aggression, good enough looks and the chutzpah that came from being the children of a car salesman had allowed them just about to coast through. John, on the other hand, had none of these things. The stunning auburn of his mother's hair and her lithe, balletic figure, both of which John's Dad had fallen for when they met, seemed to have passed him by. What was auburn in Sylvie had mutated to a pale, wan, ginger in John. Somehow, the sporting genes that had clearly jumped to his brothers had maliciously skipped around John. Generally he found himself chosen last whenever teams were picked for sport. On cross-country runs in the freezing Shropshire mist, he would drag himself round the course, lungs desperately heaving for air. On reaching the finishing line, he could hear the mocking laughter of his classmates.

The only person John can really recollect being nice to him was his Gran, his Mum's mum. She always made the time to hear his stories, serving as a voice of good-natured reason when he complained about the aloofness of his brothers and the indifference of his parents. "Come on John," she would say, "come and sit over here with your old Gran. We'll have a nice cuppa and you can tell me what's on your mind." His Gran provided a form of comfort that was so scant elsewhere.

However, she lived in London and so the time they spent together was limited, confined to the semi-annual trips from Shropshire his family would take. For John, these assumed the air of a holiday. On the car journeys down to London, he recalls his Mum being in a better mood than usual. She would sometimes talk of coming home. Had he been more perceptive, John might have noticed the simmering resentment that brewed between his parents. Sylvie, a Londoner by birth, missed the city. She tried to enthuse John about London, even if her attempts were not always successful. When hanging in a slowly rotating glass pod on the London Eye, John had felt both queasy and daunted by the size of the city. He also evokes dismal walks along the Thames, Sylvie attempting to point out landmarks, Dan generally smoking furtively a few paces behind them. He visited museums (his Mum gainfully pressing on, his Dad sneering at "stuff for clever people") and climbed hills (Primrose and Parliament), neither of which, his Dad never ceased to remind him, were as tall or as impressive as the Wrekin.

More than anything on his London visits, John looked forward to his Gran's birthday. Every year, the tradition was the same. John thinks fondly back to these occasions as he trudges to a now-empty table to pick up two half-eaten pizzas, an American Hot and a Meat Feast (John prides himself in now being able to recognise the menu's entire range). He brings to mind how his Gran and her friends always gathered in the Richmond Arms. The pub itself was fairly nondescript; a couple of streets away from the Edgware Road, but this didn't really matter. Jean had always called it her second home, a term of endearment, spoken in jest even if it belied a more fundamental truth. As far as anyone could recall, Jean and Alfred, her husband – when he had been alive – had always drunk there. So had most of their friends. The Richmond, for all of them, constituted a beacon of constancy. John can remember large crowds of people at his Gran's birthday events. Their faces blurred into one, but it was an image of warmth, not only beer-induced but heartfelt too. There were constant rounds of backslapping and pint-buying. Late arrivals were always welcomed into the fray. When John was much younger, he would generally find himself balanced on someone's knee, while songs were sung and pint glasses raised. In later years, people might chat with him, often about football, but sometimes about his school, his parents or his ambitions. For John, being here and surrounded by people who all seemed genuinely pleased to be in each other's company, who formed a community; this is what he took away. It was almost akin to a family.

And now his Gran was dead. It was all very sudden, an aneurysm. A neighbour with a spare key had found Jean collapsed on the kitchen floor, shattered cup and instant coffees granules spread around her. There was a funeral and then a wake, of course, at the Richmond Arms. Despite the drinks and sandwiches that were provided by the pub, despite Jean's favourite songs being played on the juke-box, despite the telling and retelling of anecdotes that had been repeated for the last fifty years or more, the mood felt different. It was as if a gaping hole had been left, one that could never be properly filled again. It still feels like to this John now, all the more so since he is now living in her flat. When Jean's will was opened, and it was apparent that the flat had been left to him, he was more astonished than his parents. They, it struck John, seemed almost glad to have him off their backs.

"Grown men should be able to look after themselves," was the spiteful insinuation offered by his Dad. It was followed by the snide observation, "working in the chippie down the road surely can't be your life-long ambition."

"And we'll have one less person to wash and cook for," added his mother helpfully.

"You know it makes sense, John." His Dad was never short of cliché, gleaned mostly from the tabloids.

"It will be good for you," continued his Mum, "you'll be able to make a proper living in London."

John had eventually consented to the move, hoping that the leap to London might mean some improvement in his fortunes. He would be away from his family, unburdened by the weight of their expectations and accusations and in charge of his own destiny for the first time. Life had indeed begun to look up on his first night in town. It was the idea of a large pizza that initially drew him to Perfect Pizza. He could picture it; fresh from the oven, dripping with cheese and laden with sausage. Half an hour later, belly sated, the sign in the window advertising the need for part-time employees caught his eye. He enquired, and the job was his. Those years helping in his local chippie had perhaps not been in vain.

Some things, however, had not changed. John had never really had what could be considered real friends; it was more a case of people who tolerated him, or at least didn't object actively to his presence. He would stand his round in the pub, had a passable enough knowledge of football (gleaned from the television rather than the pitch) and could hold his own conversationally. Away from Shropshire, John wondered whether life might be any different. His emotions towards the Richmond were still too confused to contemplate it as a potential local. John was unsure whether any of the regular crowd who there at his Gran's parties there would welcome him, a much younger and less confident person, into their midst. And, what would he say to them?

John was unsure. He cringed at the thought of lengthy reminiscences regarding his Gran. It wasn't that he didn't want to talk about her; more, it was that his family had never encouraged any outward expression of emotion.

Girls were an even bigger problem. John had never had a girlfriend. He felt awkward in their presence, almost as if they were an alien species. For him, girls assumed the proportion of almost supernatural beings, seemingly unattainable goddesses with long hair, unexpected curves and exotic smells. He wasn't quite sure what it would take for one of them even to notice him, let alone to engage him in conversation. Flushing as he bends to scoop a handful of festering chips off the pizza shop floor, John recalls with embarrassment a particular incident from his youth that perhaps summed up his experience. It would have been when he was still at school, but he doesn't want to think too hard when exactly. One night in his Shropshire local, senses dulled through lager, he had overheard a group of gregarious teenage girls talking in excited tones about how men who came from Wolverhampton were "well fit." John didn't know Wolverhampton and so could not assess how accurate their claims might be. However, if these girls were saying it, then he believed it *must* be true.

On a subsequent evening in a different pub, confidence fuelled by alcohol, John had spotted a pair of girls standing alone. He put on his best smile, approached beaming, and introduced himself. "Hi! I'm John, from Wolverhampton."

The girls' conversation stopped. Then, a look of blank incomprehension came over their faces. A second later, this was followed by an exchange of glances. John smiled even harder, believing the battle half-won. One of them retorted, "and so?"

John's jaw hung slack, speechless. He had not planned for this response. He realised he hadn't planned at all. His face reddened with embarrassment and he began to turn away.

"Loser!" The word rang in his ears as a peal of laugher followed from the girls. Since then, he had generally refrained from conversation with the opposite sex.

John's colleague, Abdul, was the only person who had shown any interest in him at all since he had been in London. John was grateful, but wasn't sure what to make of Abdul. Aged nineteen and back from university for the holidays, Abdul was living with his parents nearby and working at Perfect Pizza to earn some extra money. His and John's shifts often overlapped. Abdul did regularly make a point of engaging John in conversation when they were working, but always very politely refused John's entreaty to join him in the pub afterwards or on his day off. Then again, John didn't really know that much about Lebanese people and what they might do when they weren't working. He had, however, been genuinely delighted but slightly daunted when Abdul had insisted one night that he join a couple of his friends for some food after their shift ended. "Come on, you'll enjoy it; honest," Abdul had said.

Soon after they were on a bus, heading south. Beyond the Marylebone flyover John's eyes beheld a novel sight. This wasn't the London he believed he knew, and certainly not one he had ever visited with his

Gran, especially not at night. It was a riot of colour and life. Nearly all the shop frontages had signs written both in English and Arabic; fruits and vegetables were stacked in precarious piles, almost spilling out onto the street. So were the people. Large groups had congregated outside many of the cafes. When a newcomer joined, he was often hugged by the others, John observed. Some of the men were even kissing each other on the cheeks – you certainly never got that in Shropshire. Many who were seated had either small cups of coffee or tea. Others were smoking curious-looking coloured pipes. And there wasn't a pub in sight. Still somewhat in a daze, Abdul nudged John and they were off the bus, entering the Beirut Express. Abdul exchanged greetings with several people whom he knew. John felt self-conscious, but no-one's curiosity seemed aroused in the slightest by his presence. Looking around, John noted with some surprise that he wasn't the only non-Arab there. Seated on one of the stools at the counter, an Englishman was holding forth in loud tones about refugees. John spotted others too, speaking a variety of languages. He had heard Abdul proclaiming that London was a mostly welcoming city, but had not really believed him. The food was a slightly different matter.

"What's this?" John had asked when the first dishes were brought to the table.

"Baba Ghanouj, Hommos Beiruty and Mouhamara," Abdul had said.

"Yer what?" John responded.

"That one's an aubergine dip, the next is puréed chickpeas and the last is red peppers mixed with chillies and walnuts."

"Is there anything else to eat – like chips?" John had asked, bewildered by all these new words and colours, as he watched quick hands dart across the table, expertly dipping the accompanying flat breads into the dips.

"They're coming John, and some kebabs too, don't you worry. Just tuck in!"

"Er… I'm not sure. And what's that strange purple thing over there?"

"Pickled turnips – they're great; go on, you've got to give them a go!"

"Well…"

But eventually some of the sheer enthusiasm of Abdul and his friends did eventually rub off on him. He manfully sampled everything in the end, even the turnips. He didn't really know what he was eating, but he felt as if he was almost enjoying it. At least it was different to pizza. The following day he wasn't so certain. Maybe he'd over-eaten, or perhaps some of the dishes had been too spicy for him. Nonetheless, John found himself forced to visit the loo more times than he would have liked. Once he'd even had to excuse himself while at work. His colleague accepted John's request begrudgingly but told him not to take too long. At least it had been a quiet moment. No one was awaiting a take-away and only two tables were occupied, one by a group of youths in big puffa jackets and baseball caps talking in conspicuously hushed yet also rather animated tones; the other by a slightly drunken and dishevelled man in a suit munching his way disconsolately through a box of chicken wings. As John trudges back to the counter and glances up at the clock, noting that his current shift is almost over, he recalls that, *of course*, he had been away just long enough to have missed the incident that had subsequently become something of a local talking point.

While John was absent, the group of youths had got up and left the restaurant abruptly. They had only progressed a short way down the road when some sort of dispute had ensued. One thing, it seemed, had led to another; a knife was pulled and one of the group was suddenly lying bleeding on the ground. Alarms were sounded and by the time John had emerged from the bathroom, the police were already on the scene and the remaining kids long gone into the depths of the night. John had nothing to add when interviewed later by an officer. His colleague and the remaining customer had provided the police with everything they needed to know and both confirmed that John had not been present when the group departed.

Typical, thinks John, as he leaves at the end of his most recent shift, nothing exciting ever happens to him; he didn't even get to be present when the most interesting thing in months had occurred so close to where he works. Little exciting happens to John that evening either. Like most nights after his shift is over, he ambles straight out of Perfect Pizza to the Green Man. The pub offers comfortable anonymity and serves lager at a price that is just about acceptable to John. At any rate, he prefers sitting here than in his Gran's flat with a four-pack and a small bottle of cheap vodka. He'd done that on one of his first nights in London, queasily digesting his pizza, trading on memories and getting progressively more morose, not to mention drunk. One of the bartenders at the Green Man (who goes by the name of 'Rodrigo from Rio,' exuding an air of confidence and exoticism which John cannot imagine) does now recognise him, but it is little more than that, a brief exchange of pleasantries. John still harbours notions of having a conversation with someone, anyone, there. On this evening, however, he contents himself simply with lager and the highlights of the night's football games, a familiar formula.

The following day when John awakes he is assailed by several realities: of being alone in his Gran's flat (she is never returning); the relief of no work until two in the afternoon, and the fact that his heart is pounding like an overused piston. There is a dull ache in his head too. John considers that the best solution would be to have a good old fry-up. Pulling on a shabby tracksuit, he heads out of his flat, intending to go to the Metropolitan Cafe. He remembers visiting it with his Gran, being greeted by the Greek couple who used to run it. Once outside, his brain clicks into a higher gear and he is beset by disappointment. The Metropolitan, he reminds himself, shut many years ago. In its place stands somewhere called Zonzo, a posh-looking Italian restaurant. It has wine glasses and candles set on every table (a far cry from the cigarette-stained, chipped Formica tables of the Metropolitan) and offers pizzas from a wood-fired oven (something that Perfect Pizza could never claim to provide). Now, of course, the more pressing issue for John is food, and so he heads in the opposite direction towards his nearest supermarket. As he trudges onward, John thinks to himself that whatever his Mum's other failings may have been, she did teach him how to prepare a fry-up. Perhaps she had always been planning for the day when he would move out. With this thought in his mind, John barely notices at first the girl standing outside the supermarket.

She is wearing a tracksuit that is considerably cleaner than his own and, more surprisingly, is smiling broadly at him. John struggles to think when something even vaguely like this last happened. Normally, Lucy (he knows this because there is a name-badge pinned to her tracksuit) would be the sort of girl John could not imagine talking to. For a start, she is very pretty. Also, she reminds him slightly of some of the girlfriends his brothers would bring home now and then; girls they had met at university, radiating a sense of assurance and ebullience that seemed to come naturally to them, equally at home discussing netball or politics. Now, all of a sudden, she is talking to John.

"Hi there! Would you like to join Sport Central? It's twelve months' membership for the price of ten!"

"Er…?"

"Sport Central. Don't you know us? We operate the leisure centre just round the corner from here. There's a gym, squash courts, indoor football pitches, a swimming pool. Everything."

"Er. Well. Maybe."

"Here, have a leaflet."

Lucy thrusts a piece of paper into John's hand and as quickly as the exchange has begun it is over, Lucy now directing her beaming smile and perfectly pony-tailed hair at the next passer-by. John is both delighted and deflated by the exchange. He wonders, as he trundles round the shop putting food into his basket, whether he should have prolonged the conversation. What would he have said though, John muses to himself, as he pays for his items. Exiting, John hopes Lucy might look at him, remember him from their earlier meeting, but she appears deep in conversation with someone else and John does not have the courage to approach or loiter. The thought of Lucy, however, plays on John's mind throughout the rest of that day. While he is at work he entertains the idea of maybe, just maybe, taking her for dinner one day. Wouldn't that be nice? He suspects that Lucy is not the sort to be impressed by Perfect Pizza, but John thinks about Zonzo. Now that would be a classy spot, he's sure. He could ask his Dad or maybe one of his brothers what sort of wine to buy. The only problem, John considers, is how will he ever see her again? Between folding pizza boxes ahead of the anticipated evening rush, the idea comes to him. John is so excited by it that he knocks an assembled pile to the floor. Even his colleague's indignation passes him by. He has his plan. Tomorrow morning when again he is not working, he will go the sports centre. There, he will meet Lucy and it will all be OK.

When John gets home that night he picks up the leaflet Lucy gave him, hoping perhaps that there might even be a photo of her on it (little realising that she is a student at UCL, simply earning some extra money by handing out leaflets between lectures). He learns that the leisure centre is a short walk from his flat, decides to wash his clothes, refrains from drinking any beer (or no more than two cans) and even sets his alarm so he can be at the gym nice and early. Of course, things don't work out quite that way. His Gran's aged washing machine somehow manages to turn itself off in the night and therefore his clothes remain stuck in the machine, the cycle only restarting in the morning. He also sleeps through his alarm. John then realises, as he sets off down the Edgware Road wearing a Perfect Pizza polo shirt, since his other clothes are still in the wash, that he hasn't thought what he will do when he gets to the leisure centre. There are two problems, John realises. First, what will he say to Lucy if she is there? And, if she isn't, what will he do? As he gets closer, neither plan is nearer to any serious achievement. A jumble of thoughts and emotions, hopes and fears, crowd John's head. He thinks back to being picked last in school matches, he recalls all his previous failed attempts to engage girls. But then, there is the tantalising possibility that this time could be different. He is in London. No one knows him or is here to judge him. For the first time, the extent of the city and its potentially infinite possibilities seizes him. He is quite overwhelmed by this thought as he approaches the leisure centre. An almost new and certainly emboldened John pushes the door.

"Can I use the gym please?" he says cheerily to the attendant at the desk, the words springing into his head seamlessly. For a second, even Lucy is forgotten about.

"Sorry, it's closed today. The air conditioning has broken down."

In an instant, John's elation turns to deflation. It always seems to be this way; his hopes dashed, his plans foiled, his luck absent. And, of course, there is the sudden realisation that Lucy is nowhere to be seen.

"But the pool is still open."

For a moment, John is not even aware that the attendant has spoken again. "Are you a member?" she continues. "If not, it's only £2.20 if you live locally and have your Resident's Card. Otherwise, it's £6.20."

John stands momentarily like a rabbit in headlights, but realises that he is committed, that it would be more embarrassing to turn around and walk away than to do anything else. The stern lessons of childhood echo in his ears ("man-up" would be an almost daily barb thrown by his Dad). John therefore digs in his pocket and hands over the money, trying to assert with a degree of confidence that he doesn't really feel, that he *would* like to have a swim. Receipt in hand and directions provided, John heads down the corridor in the shorts that he now realises will have to double as trunks, towards the changing room. At least, he thinks, he remembered to bring a towel.

He opens the door to the changing room and takes in the scene. It is of no surprise to John that the patterned white and blue tiles are cracked in places or that a festering mould seems to cover the lower section of the door. Several of the lockers have out-of-use stickers carelessly displayed across their damaged frontage. Indeed, the whole place has seen better days. But, then again, it isn't much different to the facilities of the civic pool in Telford, a place he brings to mind with no great fondness from his time at school. He appears not to notice the unfortunate yet pervasive smell of chlorine, deodorant and general dampness. What John is more concerned about is whether he looks conspicuous and has been noticed, since he certainly *feels* conspicuous, struggling to remember the last time he voluntarily set foot in any location such as this. Apart from one man around the same age as his dad who is struggling to pull down red socks that extend above the knee, no one pays John a bit of notice. Red-sock man gives him a nosy look, but then returns to the task in hand. Elsewhere, it is business as usual. Bags are being unpacked or packed, shirts discarded, flesh towelled and abs flexed. There is the whine of a hair dryer, a fragment of a conversation about how one of the toilets is out of order again, another about the football he watched a couple of nights ago. Taking a further look around as he proceeds towards the bench where he places his bag, John notices what a varied lot the people seem to be here: young and old, black and white, fit and unhealthy. To his left, John sees a man of muscular proportions of which he could only dare dream. A look of apparent anger clouds his face and John decides not to let his glance linger for too long. Within his vision he also takes in sagging bellies, varicose veins, tattooed bodies and fading suntans. Perhaps, John considers, he may not be so different. Clothes off, he pads towards a locker that is within easy reach, top-left on the first bank, key number 100 in its socket. He inserts his coin, twists the lock, struggles to attach the wristband to his arm and waddles off in the direction of the pool, a sensation of trepidation pervading. Somewhere behind him, amid the noise of the dryer, the whir of the air conditioning and the fragments of conversation, John hears a plummy and somewhat cryptic exclamation ring out: "Bert won't be happy." Not knowing or really caring all that much what this may mean, John plods on towards the pool. At this stage, he feels, it is too late to turn back.

BERT

Bert is happy. He has been having the same dream that has regularly populated his recent sleep. In it, sunlight flickers like a thousand jewels on the placid lake in front of them. He and Iris can feel the warmth on their backs as they gaze out over the beautiful scene of blue water in the foreground, green pastures further ahead and white mountain peaks in the distance. There are the sounds of children contentedly playing nearby, the engine motor of a steamer ploughing its stately way across the water. Beside them is set a picnic rug, red and white checked. On it is spread fresh bread, cheese, sausage and a couple of bottles of beer. Bert announces to Iris that he is going to go for a swim. She looks at him radiantly and tells him to go ahead. She says she will just rest and enjoy the view. As he plunges into the water, the spray fresh on his face, Iris' laughter in the background, he is suddenly pulled through layers of sleep into the present day. There is the realisation that Iris is now dead; and, also, that the events of their honeymoon about which he has been dreaming, yet can recall with the same clarity as if they were yesterday, occurred over fifty years ago. The other realisation, and the more pressing problem, is that Bert can't remember what he did yesterday, or even which day of the week it is.

The world has recently become a much more frightening place for Bert. Daily, it is more of a struggle for Bert to understand what is going on around him. Not that he wants to admit it. Nonetheless, there seem to be fewer constants and more changes. Bert finds himself regularly returning to the past, since the present is so very confusing. Besides, it is easier. He is suddenly reminded for some reason of the comment made by that smart-arsed doctor whom he went to see not that long ago. It was something to do with books and bookcases. He hadn't been able to get a word in edgeways, to tell the quack he wasn't much of a reading sort of person; and yet the man had continued to prattle on. Anyway, the doctor's idea went something along the lines that if you were to tip the case over, then the books at the top would fall out before those at the bottom. That was bloody obvious, thought Bert. Scarily though, this was apparently what was happening to his memories; the more recent ones were disappearing, but those lodged at the back of his brain, or at the bottom of the bookshelf, would stay with him for longer. He doesn't want to think too hard about the doctor's depressing diagnosis at this moment and so instead revisits the memories of his dream and that holiday he had with Iris.

They had been planning a trip to the seaside, since they were getting married. Perhaps it would be Clacton. Or maybe Margate; he'd heard it was posher. He'd saved up some of money. It wasn't much, but then he didn't earn an awful lot selling fruit and veg at the market on Church Street. Like all his mates back then, Bert was a football fan. He did the pools religiously every week. It was a bit of fun, obviously not as good as going to the game, but you could still *imagine* what it was like, the shouting of the crowds, the action, the excitement. On the particular day that he now focuses on, he had his pink betting slip with the black grid in his pocket, the boxes crossed, the home win for United marked, the away win for Spurs, the score-draw for City and so on. When he heard the results, he had checked them against those he had predicted, checked them for a second time just to make sure. He can recall almost dropping his slip with excitement. He didn't want to tell any of his mates before he'd told Iris, but he had got 23 points. Anything more than 21 was good enough to share part of the pool's pay-out that day. That would mean a lot of money; they could have whatever honeymoon they wanted. It was about £60 in the end, the equivalent of almost three months' work at the market. Iris – who had always been the decisive one – knew immediately where they should go. "Come on Bert, let's go to Austria!" she had exclaimed enthusiastically.

They had both been to watch *The Sound of Music* at the cinema earlier that year. He hadn't enjoyed it all that much, although he had liked to see the Nazis getting their come-uppance at the film's end. They deserved it. However, Iris had fallen in love with the film almost immediately, from the opening scenes of the mountain tops stretching as far as the eye could see through to the infectious enthusiasm of Maria. She was singing the songs for weeks after. Even now, the sound of her reciting the words of "Do-Re-Mi" rings with absolute clarity in his mind. The travel agent they had gone to see hadn't been able to book them on a trip to the Austrian Alps at such short notice. "How about Switzerland?" he had suggested.

Before Bert could express an opinion, he remembers Iris pressing his hand with excitement: "What fun Bert – let's do it! We'll be just like the von Trapp family, running away on an adventure," she had said. What a holiday it had been too. Bert recollects it all perfectly. He pictures the trains that always ran on time, the little yellow buses that sounded their horns as they swung round precipitous mountain corners, the taste of the chocolate and the milk, his hand in hers, the two of them together. They had gone for walks, had picnics, visited quaint castles, taken boats on lakes.

Still happy, his mind wanders further back, to a time before Iris. He believes his first distinct memory is of Christmas. It would have been 1949 or 1950, he reckons, and a few days before 25 December. At the time, of course, there was no electricity, certainly not in his house, and not even on most of the streets. Instead, the gas man would come by on his pushbike in the evening and fire up the street lights. That day though, as he had turned from his home on to Church Street, it was like stepping into an Aladdin's cave, or some other fairy tale. All the stallholders had decorated their pitches with coloured lights. They glistened and sparkled. It was a rare splash of colour and excitement in what had been a time of mostly grey hardship. He had skipped through the market and then into Taylor's the Confectioner to spend the money he had been given – "go on Bert, here's a couple of pennies, it's your Christmas treat," his Dad had said. He can still recall the rows of jars of brightly coloured boiled sweets, the indecision of which ones to choose, the calculations of how many his pennies might buy him. Or instead, maybe he might have a lemonade. They did fizzy drinks there, which they made from a powder, the drink turning bright yellow as you added the water. Further down the street was Chocolate Joe's, where they also sometimes used to go, although Bert did not like it so much. He had always been faintly frightened by Joe, the owner, and the hammer that he would wield to break big blocks of chocolate into pieces.

Other memories from back then crowd his thoughts as he lies in bed that morning, seeking the courage to face another day. He thinks of circus animals, camels and zebras, big and exotic, being led down the street on their way to the music hall on the Edgware Road; also, about the death of a stammering King, when the shop windows had all been dressed in purple, as a form of commemoration. Bert wishes he or his parents had taken some photos of these events, but few people he knew had cameras back then. It was not like today, when the young kids he sees on the streets seem to be snapping away at everything with their new-fangled smart phone thingies.

Now it is all different. The old shops have all gone. So have many of the boozers where he used to drink. He remembers Davies Dairy with the two sheepdogs that would stand guard outside, where he would be sent on regular errands; additionally, Murray's the Butchers from where they would sometimes get hot saveloys and pease pudding at the weekends when they wanted to splash out. Neither was there any longer. Nor was Giljay's, where he had bought some of his first records at the time when Beatlemania was just beginning, the sounds of John, Paul, George and Ringo still fresh in everyone's ears. Jordan's too, where he and Iris had got things for their house, from curtains to crockery, had shut. On almost every street where he looked the shells of former pubs lingered, now converted to other uses or simply left boarded-up and derelict. The Duke of York had been an Indian restaurant for years while the Hero of Maida had turned into some poncey skin care clinic. Now, there would never be another chance to eat jellied eels at the Duke of Clarence. It had long since shut down, as had Tubby Isaac's fish stall on the market, from which the pub used to get its eels. He had started to make lists – of the stalls and shops in Church Street, the pubs in the local area, of things that used to be there, but were no longer. It was a way of remembering rather than forgetting. He goes everywhere with his notebook now.

Bert isn't quite sure when it had first started to happen. He had never been the sharpest tool in the box, but in recent conversations he would struggle to find the right words for things. There had been that time in the pub recently. He'd wanted to have a sit down.

"Oi, Roger! Pass me that…" The word had been on the tip of his tongue, the image in his mind, but it had then danced cruelly away. "That…thing you sit on."

"Righty-ho, Bert. There's your chair."

And then later he'd said to Ernie, "here, pass me your book; I want to take a look at the horses."

"What book, Bert?" was Ernie's response.

"What's that you're reading Ern?"

"Oh, my paper! You want a peek at that?"

"Yup, book, paper – it's all the same to me."

"Here you are Bert. But mind how you go. Sounds like you've been at the beer a bit too much!"

Ernie had laughed, as did some of the others. Bert had joined in – reluctantly – even though he knew that alcohol wasn't the problem; it was more than that.

Bert has a feeling of impotent frustration, not something he can find a proper way of describing. It is almost as if he were constantly trying to grasp at things, catch them, but instead finding them elusively just out of reach. When he sits down to watch telly in the evening, he finds his mind wandering, he struggles to concentrate and even recall what has happened just a few minutes ago. Now that Iris has gone, he has to do all the paperwork. But every time he's at the table, the gas bill or something like that in front of him, the numbers swim and make no sense. He had cooked for a while after Iris' death and even quite enjoyed it, but now following a recipe is often too complicated. Instead he is increasingly making do with microwave meals. Sometimes he still manages the trip to the Church Street Cafe. He is comforted by the familiarity of its black and white tiled floor, its red walls and low ceiling. The market traders continue to come in for their carry-outs, but he can linger there over a brew. And they do an excellent roast with three veg for not much more than six quid.

The problem is that there is almost no one Bert can talk to about his fleeting thoughts and disappearing memories. His life, he feels, is becoming characterised by an increasing sense of loneliness. Iris, for long his rock, has been dead now some years – eight he thinks it is. The cancer had got her in the end, gradually eating at her until Iris had finally given in and faded away, her bones prominent and her skin the colour of old parchment. They had never had children. Not that they

33

hadn't tried, but things like fertility treatment weren't around when he and Iris had been younger. It had been a struggle at the time to mask the disappointment they felt, almost a failure of some sort, particularly when yet another of their friends had announced they were having a baby. He felt that Iris had suffered more than him, but they had never really talked that much about it, you didn't so much back then. By some sort of mutual yet unspoken agreement, the topic of adoption was never brought up, while the idea of making a baby in a test tube made no sense at all to them. Bert had worried for a while that there might be something wrong with his seed, but somehow he never got round to going to see anyone about it, constantly making convenient excuses and justifications to himself. As time had passed, the anguish had diminished, but it was still there, filed away in a special place at the back of his mind combined with the aching knowledge that there would be no heirs – potentially even no one – left to remember the impact he had on their lives. Bert's friends are now also gradually dropping, one by one: William and Ronald both gone too with cancer; Stevie from Parkinson's; Alf, his best mate, from a heart attack, and of course Alf's wife Jean most recently from… now, what was the word? He did know it somewhere; something to do with a swelling of blood… yes, that was right, an aneurysm.

At least there are still some constants. The Richmond Arms is unchanging. When he and Iris had moved into a flat in Dicksee House that the council had found them not long after getting married (it had been a relief no longer having to share with Iris' parents and her siblings), he had joked to his friends how his dream had come true. He

34

had always wanted to live a stone's throw away from a pub, and now here they were. And those who remained from the gang back then would still congregate in the Richmond. The place hadn't received a lick of paint in many years, nor the carpet a clean. Both were stained, through excesses of tobacco and alcohol. It was cold throughout the seasons and the beer, by contrast, was generally warm. But none of this mattered. This was their local. Many of the guys would come in here when the place opened, now that they weren't working, and perhaps stay until it shut. They would nurse their pints slowly, poring over the newspaper, analysing the racing form. They might hobble out to go to the bookies, or perhaps to do some shopping, but you could generally count on Ernie or Ned, Florence and Roger still being there. If they weren't, then they might be at the Lord High Admiral. Bert sometimes goes there too, since it is by the market, but it has never been his local. There are, of course, fewer birthdays to attend at the Richmond now. Historically, these had been major events, friends and family, cousins and children coming along, the beer often flowing from the afternoon through until closing time. Each one that occurs is still celebrated, but the occasions are now marked more as a form of achievement, the sense that another year had been survived, a series of increasingly challenging hurdles overcome. The old guard who remain, faithful through to the end, have retained the tradition of round-buying, though of course they are now much smaller in size. Bert and the others have all become increasingly aware that their time is running out, draining gradually away.

Still, Bert continues to make the effort to be healthy, to keep himself in shape. He had decided a while back not to let himself go, like some of the others. Maybe it was the discipline that had been imposed by his parents in the years after the War when he was growing up. Treats were few and far between and many things, such as bacon, were literally rationed until he would have been about ten. There had always been fruit at least. He can never really recall a time without it. The market traders on Church Street would always have an apple or orange to spare for the kids, even in those years of austerity. There was a proper sense of community back then. Everyone looked out for each other.

It was Terry, Alf's dad, who had first let Bert work on his stall after school and at the weekends to earn a few extra pennies. Initially, it was his job to break up the empty wooden boxes that had contained the produce. These would be bundled up and could be sold for kindling. Later, when he was bigger, Bert would accompany Terry in his van to Covent Garden Market to pick up the goods. The early morning starts – wonderful in summer, the street deserted except for the sight of seagulls feasting eagerly on discarded waste; a lot harder in winter, the morning still pitch black and bitterly cold – all of it remains etched in his mind. So too is the recollection of when he first got his own stall, the sense of pride that accompanied it and he carried with him for weeks after. It is something he still feels now, as he summons up the memories again. It was always hard work, but a lot of fun, a good way of making an honest living. He liked the routine, the banter – "three punnets for a pound, get your lovely strawberries here!" or "oi, where you get them cucumbers from; off the back of a lorry?!" – the camaraderie, the shared experiences and the common endeavour. He had carried on for as long as he could. It wasn't that his health was failing him. No, he had felt as fit as a fiddle. It was more that he was struggling to summon up the same enthusiasm as he had felt when he was younger. Like with everything else, the market had begun to change too. Moroccan, Kurdish and other foreign stallholders had begun to occupy pitches. They brought with them their own produce, things Bert had never seen before, herbs and spices with names he couldn't pronounce properly. They spoke a different language and formed their own community. Many liked it, and there was certainly more colour in the market than ever before, but it just wasn't how it used to be.

That is why Bert clings to his memories, sometimes almost desperately, much like a man drowning might try to retain his hold on a piece of driftwood, or anything solid. Small things and routine help, he finds. On his morning walk, the seagulls wheeling around the market act as a comforting presence, their echoing calls constituting a form of reassurance, a reminder of normality. Seagulls had always been part of his life: they had been there on his first walks round the corner to school as a child; they were still there in his later years working in the market. On almost every holiday he had ever been on, seagulls had been present too, as much part of the British seaside as beaches, donkey rides and sticks of rock. He recalls, even now, Iris laughing at him when he had pointed out to her that they hadn't seen a single seagull in Switzerland. "Of course not, silly", she had countered,

"Switzerland doesn't have any coast, and it would be a long way for them to fly from the sea."

Yes, Iris always did know things. Although she'd worked as a char, right since school she had always been interested in learning. She'd cleaned houses in Notting Hill, mostly occupied by young City types as she called them. Sometimes she had helped at their parties in the evenings too, coming back with stories of extravagance which he could barely imagine, the empty bottles piled up in the kitchen along with enormous platters of discarded seafood. She would often marvel at how grand their houses were, how they were full of paintings, books and the like. Sometimes Iris would take a peek at the books. This was how she had impressed him one day with the fact she had gleaned – by chance, from flicking through a large glossy catalogue on art during a tea break at so-and-so's flat – that the block where they lived was named after some painter. Apparently, he had been quite well known in his time. Not long after this, Iris had suggested a trip one Sunday to the Tate since she had read that some of his pictures were there. Amidst all the gold frames, the long corridors, the hushed voices, he had felt far from his comfort zone. The cinema or the pub were more his thing, but he recalls Iris' sense of joy when they had finally worked out which room contained the art by Sir Francis Dicksee, her exclamation of "just picture that, we live in a house named after him." Maybe the postcard she had bought was still around somewhere. Bert knows though that he will never go back to the art gallery. He would be lost without Iris.

Bert feels her void constantly. He wishes she were still here. She would know what to do about the cotton wool that now seems to be filling his head, the cloud of haze that is forming around him. It was Iris who had always taken care of practical things. After Bert had given up his pitch at the market, she had been the one to insist on him developing some sort of structure in his day.

"That's the way to stay young and fit," she had said. Not that the advice had worked for her, Bert thinks bitterly, recalling how the cancerous cells had spread their evil path from her lungs onward. Nonetheless, at the time she had sat him down at their kitchen table and told him that he needed to think about what he really enjoyed doing. Bert had been a bit stumped. The market was pretty much all he had ever known. Iris had pressed on. "Now Bert," she had said, "while you were never one for lessons back at school, what about sport? You were pretty good, in the team for football and cricket. And then there was swimming too. What about that? Why not start using the pool again?"

What Iris said was true. Back in his youth Bert had shown promise in the water, had even swum in a couple of competitions. The big pool at the Baths, as Bert still calls the local leisure centre, no longer existed. Times had moved on. The pool had been covered over, the spectator stands disassembled. In their place now was some sort of artificial surface, where people would play indoor football or sometimes badminton. When he visits now, as he does most days – Iris' suggestion having been heeded, and still adhered to, even in her absence – Bert often wonders whether any of the youngsters kicking a ball around ever realise that they are standing on top of a disused pool. He sometimes considers telling some of the lads in the changing room the story, but fears it might not come out quite right, that it might be considered as simply the deranged ravings of an old man. He could also mention the days when people would come to the Baths to wash either themselves or their clothes, sometimes both. There had originally been washing troughs and machines, drying horses and irons too. All this seemed a world away now.

However, Bert enjoys the swimming. He likes the routine (Iris had been right), seeing mostly the same faces in the changing room, partaking a bit in the chatter, and then entering the water. It has neither the cold salty tang he associates with the seaside, nor the bracing freshness that the lakes in Switzerland had. But floating there in the Edgware Road Baths, freed from the constraints of gravity as well as time, Bert finds himself returning to these memories, of happier times. In the water, he is able escape, and does not have to confront any of the challenges posed by the outside world. The slow yet rhythmic pace of lengths is relaxing, peaceful and restful. Up and down, up and down, Bert would go. A bit like a goldfish. After each length, Bert would sometimes have to force himself to remember what he had started to think about at the beginning. Sometimes he could; others times he couldn't. A bit like a goldfish.

The doctor had at least been pleased when Bert mentioned that he tried to make it to the pool every day. Regular exercise was good for his condition, he had been told. One day he had finally plucked up the courage and made an appointment. Or rather, Jean had made it for him. Bert had eventually confided in her. It was she who had talked sense into him, just like Iris would have done. So, he'd gone across the road to the local medical centre. His usual doctor wasn't available for some reason, so Bert was seen by a young chap. He had listened politely to what Bert told him, yet had refused to make eye contact for any length of time. Instead, he had taken refuge in glancing regularly at his computer screen. Occasionally, he would sneak a look at his watch too, hoping that Bert would not notice. But he did. Finally, the doctor had spoken to Bert earnestly, trying not to use long words, but confusing him nonetheless. He had tried patiently (but not patiently enough) to explain that Bert had some sort of dementia, most probably Alzheimer's. It wasn't certain. They would have to do some tests. There was no cure, the doctor had said; it still wasn't even clear why people got the disease, but there were some drugs that might slow the condition down. He had then turned to his computer to print out a few forms before walking to his filing cabinet to get Bert a bunch of leaflets, still failing to meet his eye. When he had walked down the stairs and out of the medical centre, clutching uselessly at his glossy pamphlets, Bert wasn't sure how he felt. More than anything, he wanted a drink. As he sat in the Richmond, defiantly disregarding the doctor's suggestion that alcohol should be consumed in moderation, emotions of anger, disbelief and sheer terror began to fill him. More than anything though, it was an abiding sense of loneliness which he felt. He would have to face his inevitable descent alone.

The visit to the doctor had been a few months ago, Bert reckons, though he is not exactly sure. He had ignored the offer of another appointment and had decided not to take any tests. He didn't want to mess around with any drugs that might make him even more confused.

No, he would carry on for as long as he could without help. What would be, would be, Bert thinks. Some days are good, others much less so. The worst thing, Bert finds, are the hallucinations. The doctor had said it was possible that he might get these, but recently they seemed to have been appearing with increasing regularity. He sometimes feels as if everything is unravelling; it is like… trying to put the spool back into one of those small plastic thingies he has that plays music; yes, that's right now, it's on the tip of his tongue now… a cassette.

The strange images he sees seem to crop up in the oddest of places. When he was brushing his teeth only the other day, he had been convinced for a moment that his old Dad had been there in the room right behind him. But this, surely, wasn't possible since his death had occurred more than twenty years ago. Bert had paused, brush in hand, turned around, then back to the mirror. It then dawned on him that it must have been his reflection. Yet the image had stayed with him all day. Once there he somehow couldn't manage to get rid of it. On another recent occasion, he had been watching TV. *Mary Poppins* had been showing. He swore he knew the woman in it. Of course, it was Jean. Everyone had always said that she was the pretty one, the one who looked like Julie Andrews. The four of them – Bert and Alf, Iris and Jean – always used to hang out together, watching shows at the Metropolitan Music Hall and later at the Odeon by Marble Arch, eating ice creams after at the Regent's Milk Bar, as thick as thieves. Everyone always said that he and Alf had done well, although Alf probably better – he had got the looker, and Bert the sensible one, people remarked. Yet, it couldn't be Jean on the telly, since she was dead, and so were

Iris and Alf. Everything was a muddle, a jumble. Sometimes when he went to get his coat from the hook by the door, he would imagine that Alf or maybe one of the others had called round, was waiting for him. As he approached, words would fail him, and the vision would melt into a much more mundane reality. It was just his coat hanging there, empty and lifeless. Worse, the blue tiles on his kitchen floor would sometimes take on the impression of water, the image of a lake or pool swimming before his eyes.

As he walks to the Baths later that morning, having managed to get dressed, pick up his swimming towel, wallet too, and lock the door (he had begun to leave post-it notes around the house; necessary prompts, but they did help), Bert is haunted by one particular fragment of semi-memory again. By now, he isn't sure whether it is real or just imagined, another one of his funny hallucinations. However, the police tape and the yellow metal boards appealing for information are still there, serving as a constant reminder that something obviously *did* happen that evening.

He had been at home, had had trouble focusing on anything and thought a walk might clear his head. He had ended up in the Lord High Admiral, had bumped into an old chum there, and one pint had turned into several. Bert thinks he remembers leaving the pub, but has no idea what time it would have been. As he had lumbered slowly up the Edgware Road, he had passed a bunch of youths. They were tall lads, all dark skinned, packed together in a tight bunch. Trying to picture the scene clearly now is hard. When he had been their age, there weren't so many non-whites around. Old Windrush Bob, as he was known, had lived just round the corner from him when he was a kid. He had been something of a local celebrity back then, a novelty, a man full of different stories. Maybe these kids were his children, or perhaps his grandchildren. None of it made any sense. Maybe they were friends of Bob's. But friends didn't argue, not like these boys seemed to be doing. Their anger radiated. Bert had hurried on, not even looking back when the sound of police sirens began to ring out. There were always sirens in the area, it was part of the pattern of daily life, almost as familiar as the seagulls, but a lot less comforting.

The days after, everyone had talked about a murder, a teenager stabbed on the street. In the Richmond, at the pool's changing room, everywhere, it seemed to be the main topic of conversation. Things like this didn't happen every day. Bert wasn't sure what to contribute, so he just kept quiet. That was certainly one of the problems with his illness, he was becoming less confident. He's uncertain if any of it would make sense if he tried to describe what he *thinks* he saw that evening. The events of that night had taken on an almost dream-like quality; maybe, Bert reflects, he didn't see anything; he is just getting it all mixed up with something he watched on the box the other day. He certainly hadn't been to the police. The police station, ugly and imposing, was very nearby, standing where the Music Hall used to be. But he had always disliked coppers. Working on the market, it had almost become ingrained to be wary of them. His was a cash business; things sometimes did fall off the back of lorries, favours needed to be asked, and then repaid. Strangers who suddenly appeared for a drink in his locals, particularly the Lord High Admiral, were always considered to be part of the Old Bill, on the prowl for information. Anyway, he wasn't going to go to the police; they might think him a lunatic, they might even suggest he go into a care home of some sort, where someone could look after him better, and he certainly wasn't having that.

Nonetheless, the event had shaken him. It continues to play back in his mind, now confused together with other thoughts, images and memories. The past and the present were becoming mixed together into some form of murky soup. Bert hopes that the swim will help clear his mind. His hands are shaking as he enters the changing room that day. Around him Bert sees faces and bodies. They are all merging into one mass of flesh. Clothes and towels are scattered everywhere in a mess. Perhaps he is back at school, and these are his friends; there they all are, getting ready for a competition. But that can't be possible. He would be excited, and now all he feels is a sense of deep-seated fear, a thing to which he can't put any words.

Then, the mist clears, at least a little. Bert makes out some people he thinks he recognises, not that he can evoke any of their names today. There is the young lad who's covered in tattoos and speaks with an accent that certainly isn't English; nearby is another regular, the large black man, who has a particularly angry scowl on his face today. He can see a couple of older guys he thinks he recognises in the distance, hunched and laboured in their movements. They're generally in the same lane as him in the water, aged vessels passing each other. And, leering right in front of him, or so it seems, is that know-it-all man, the one who's always got an opinion on this or that, who seems to be familiar with everyone and everything. "Good morning Bert", his rich voice peals out.

"What's good about this morning?" wonders Bert.

"Some young lad's stolen your locker, I'm afraid", the man continues.

The confusion shows on Bert's face for a moment. Which is his locker? It doesn't have a sticker with his name on it. Then he remembers. That's the reason he chose number 100, the top left on the furthest bank. It's the one closest to the pool. He would always be able to find it on his way back after his swim. Bert shrugs at Archie – the name of the man suddenly popping into his head. What is there to say? Life is too short, he has more important things to worry about. A few minutes later, Bert has changed. In his faded trunks, he walks towards the pool, looking forward to the water and the calm he hopes it may bring to his troubled mind. Maybe if he tries hard enough – or just lets go – he will find himself transported back to the lakes of Switzerland again. Yes, he was happy there.

ARCHIE

Archie is humming. It is a piece by Vaughan Williams, 'The Lark Ascending,' which he had heard on the radio that morning. It puts him in a good mood, at least temporarily. The tune makes him think about flight, about escaping. Archie imagines himself as the bird, whirling ever higher in a clear blue sky, getting away from everything. The soaring melodies of the tune are on his lips as he cycles to the station that morning. They reappear at several moments throughout his day. Archie knows that his humming is something of an affectation, but it calms him down, helping to take his mind off other things. It also greatly irritates his wife, which is partly why he does it. Anything is easier than talking to her.

His reveries about flight and freedom are interrupted by the sour memory of the most recent dispute that he had with Georgina earlier this morning before leaving the house.

"Archibald" (she called him this only when angry), "you're avoiding me and the children. Why do you have to leave so early? You're running away not only from your family, but your responsibilities too."

Archie knew she was correct (she always was) and further that this was not just a pointless argument, but an unwinnable one too. She, rather than he, should have gone into the law, Archie had thought ruefully. Nonetheless, he responded doggedly.

"Georgie" (his term of endearment for her, even though she detested it), "you *know* the reason. It's because I want to go swimming."

"Yes. But, why do you need to do it in such a convoluted way? It's ridiculous that you choose to swim in some grotty pool that's nowhere near either your home or your work, just because you're sentimentally attached to it for some absurd reason."

"But Georgie…"

"There are no 'buts' Archibald! What would make much more sense – and you know it too – would be for you to have breakfast with me and *our* children, and for you to find a swimming pool much closer to your office or our home. Why not consider that lovely one at the golf club?"

Archie often found that the best strategy was denial; a pretence that he had not heard her, or preferably that the debate had never occurred. "Got to go, dear. The exercise will do me good. We can talk later."

"Archibald! How dare you ignore me like this, particularly when you *know* that you're in the wrong."

Rather than responding, Archie resorted to humming valiantly, consciously choosing to ignore the air of resentment that had settled on the household. It was the second time this week that they had had a similar dispute.

He struggles to remember when it was that he fell out of love with Georgina. Maybe they had never really been in love. Many people had been surprised when they had got married, for Georgina had never had any shortage of suitors, given both her looks and her family's standing. He is more surprised that their marriage has endured nineteen years. The main (or perhaps only) thing which had originally been in Archie's favour was that he had struck up a close friendship with Magnus, her brother. They were university chums. Additionally, their post-student lives had initially developed along reasonably parallel tracks, although these had long since diverged. At the time, Archie had perhaps reminded Georgina in some way of her brother, the two sharing many interests, from classical music to sport. This was probably what had drawn her and Archie together. Magnus had been best man at their wedding.

All Archie feels now, however, is that his marriage has become one long indissoluble misery, with any trace of emotion between them thoroughly suppressed. Their sex life, which had been quite sparse even in the early days of their marriage, has now dwindled into almost non-existence. Back then he had wondered whether Georgina liked sex at all. He still ponders this matter now. They had long ceased sharing a bed, an arrangement which looks unlikely ever to change. Archie is constantly conscious of having somehow let Georgina down, an impression which perhaps dates to that moment in their early marriage, a time about by which they no longer speak. Nonetheless, his sense of having botched things has undoubtedly developed over time, evolving, mutating and crowding out almost all other feelings. The reasons for her apparent displeasure have never been formally enumerated. It is nothing that she has ever specifically said to him; more the way she just *looks* at him, sometimes wistfully, almost longingly, but always with a certain sense of regret, he feels. Maybe it is because he still works at the same firm of solicitors; that they haven't had as many children as she had perhaps wanted; that they don't yet have the house in the south of France or the chalet in the Alps that some of their friends possess.

Whatever it is, there is some crucial element missing in their relationship. At times, it feels akin to a dull ache or a nagging pain; more often though, it appears to Archie as a riddle for which there is apparently no answer.

Sometimes Archie cannot help but compare himself to Magnus. After university (he had gone down with a First, in contrast to the Upper Second gained by Magnus, a notable minor victory to which Archie still clings proudly) they had both decided to begin their careers in the legal profession and were articled at the same firm, Crispin, Keagan & Smith, a middling establishment located near Lincoln's Inn. At the time, Archie had had lofty visions of winning over sceptical juries and impressing judges with impassioned arguments based on well-grounded reason and logic. He had even believed that he might eventually graduate one day to a level where he would be one of the mighty, able to dispense justice and make wise pronouncements from his position of elevated seniority. Yet whereas Magnus had gone on to make a name for himself, moving rapidly up the ladder at Crispin's before being poached by a more distinguished rival firm, and then eventually setting up his own practice in Cheltenham, Archie had continued to plod valiantly along. Much of his early experience had been in the unprestigious field of representing clients on Legal Aid. His role had not evolved significantly since then. Internal vacancies with the promise of a promotion and new challenges did come along and were applied for, but Archie always found himself rejected, the reasons left mostly unclear. Perhaps he just wasn't very good at his job, not forceful or dynamic enough. Yet Archie continued with it, still dutifully developing the same lengthy discourses, opining in the courts and winning most but by no means all of his cases. He had long since given up applying for new roles, resigning himself to mediocrity, still broadly believing in justice, social order and other such worthy causes, if not career progression.

Archie often evokes his university days with fondness. In his mind's eye, this was a golden period, full of promise. Everything was much simpler then, before work, marriage and children – real life. Initially, Archie had been somewhat overwhelmed by Oxford. Diligence and application at his grammar school near Dorking had seen him win a scholarship. His proud parents had driven him up to St Edmund's Hall, had helped carry his meagre possessions to his room and had even joined him for a welcome tea with the Provost. Then he was abandoned, left surrounded by boys inherently more confident and at home than he, trunks bearing their initials long since installed and unpacked in their rooms, college scarves already worn complacently around their necks. Luckily his next-door neighbour in halls – Magnus – had taken Archie under his wing. It had helped that they were both studying law, and what Magnus offered in terms of the confidence and worldliness that his upbringing had provided for him (of course, he had been schooled at Eton) was compensated for by Archie's more dogged devotion to and persistence in the study of their chosen subject. Archie had been a quick learner and soon found himself comfortably immersed not just in the gilded reading rooms of the college library, but equally in the lingua franca of college life; when it was required to wear subfusc, how regularly battels had to be paid and what was the correct amount of work to put in for collections. The donning of black tie soon became almost commonplace, as did talk of Formal Hall dinners and Commemorative Balls. Archie still has wistful thoughts about the way the early evening sunlight would fall on Oxford, casting a mellow hue across the city, rendering the imposing buildings like stately beings, their watchful presence enduring and unchanging throughout time. He had loved Oxford in all weathers, cycling around the city, across cobbled streets and down hidden alleys, appreciating both its history and his place in its ever-exciting present. Summers were associated with punting and picnics by the river; winters were for bracing walks and pints by a toasting pub fire.

In contrast, when Archie considers his current home in Moor Park, he finds it hard to conjure up any affection for this private estate nestling on the far boundaries of Betjeman's Metroland. It was Georgina, with her innate sense of practicality (and the help of some of her family's money), who had concluded that Moor Park was an expedient and appropriate option, neither too far from the city nor the countryside. He recalls being told of the good schools for their undoubtedly soon-pending offspring in the vicinity, and the very nice local golf club which offered an excellent programme of social events and good networking opportunities. For Archie, it had represented the worst of all worlds; neither London nor the nearby Chiltern Hills. Nothing had changed his opinion since then. If there were a community here, then it was a gated one; neighbours generally keeping their lives private and only deigning to talk to each other if there were some advantage to be gained, often when needing to explain the potential disturbance that may occur when yet another extension was being built. It was a place with no reverence for the past and a present existence which was characterised by shuttered sterility. The future seemed equally bleak; each new family who arrived erected an ever-higher perimeter fence around their own personal fiefdom, a plethora of security cameras trained on fleets of expensive parked cars.

This is why Archie likes his visits to the swimming pool. He revels in the anonymity the place provides; no one knows him here and he is free to express his opinions – which he does unreservedly – safe in the knowledge that any judgement made about him will not reverberate to his wife, neighbours or colleagues. Further, the people at the pool are an antidote to those with whom he works, as well as to the dullards at the local golf club and the socially climbing parents whose conversation he is forced to endure at his children's school fêtes. Here, he is not mediocre, far from it. Archie tries not to judge his fellow pool-goers, but implicitly does. He finds them interesting, but looks down on them (not that he would ever openly admit this). Wherever possible Archie seeks to demonstrate in his exchanges what he feels to be his superior level of intelligence. At the pool, Archie encounters builders, train drivers, pensioners, students and more. Combined, their presence and the ensuing conversation provide a myriad of cultural references, opinions and stories for Archie. Naturally, he contributes too: "Anyone here a Vaughan Williams fan? I was only listening to him this morning on the radio. A wonderful composer." Or: "Football? Rather a boorish game. Now cricket, that's a much more civilised sport, especially the five-day form."

Magnus had been the one who introduced Archie to the leisure centre many years ago. When they had both first been working in London, their shared love of sport had helped to keep them close, although their lives were already beginning to drift apart. This passion dated back to university. Archie and Magnus had both made the college Second Eight for rowing. They had done respectably, earning their bumps once in Torpids. At cricket too, the pair had been solidly dependable opening spinners, often flummoxing opposition sides and carrying the match. In London, opportunities in a boat, or to don whites, were somewhat few and far between, but there were still ample chances for them to continue their long-standing squash duels. Archie was a technically better player, he felt, but Magnus was undoubtedly physically stronger. Magnus generally won. While Archie had initially settled in to a studio flat close to his law firm that seemed to account for almost all his monthly salary, Magnus had benefited from the use of his family's London pied-à-terre, a not-so-small dwelling just off Marylebone High Street. Even though the journey to the leisure centre had been clearly more arduous for Archie than it was for Magnus, and even if Archie had generally been the instigator, he always looked forward to their meetings: the squash, a refreshing swim after and then perhaps an ale or two, if Magnus was in the mood.

Their squash games had ceased long ago. Magnus had been in Cheltenham for a decade now, almost certainly with new squash partners and better courts nearby. Not that Archie has ever used them. Indeed, were it not for Georgina, he and Magnus might well have lost all contact. When they do still meet at enforced family gatherings – the christenings, the weddings, the funerals – Archie typically finds himself adopting an act of self-aggrandisement, exaggerating his prospects at work and their plans for the house, much to Georgina's barely veiled irritation.

"Archie! What a treat, a '96 Lafite. But really, surely a little punchy for a midweek meal with your old brother-in-law," Magnus had said when they had last met – some months ago.

"Anything for you Magnus. It's only appropriate to celebrate seeing you."

"Things must be going well at Crispin's. Are they paying you properly – at last? I didn't think they handed out serious bonuses there. They certainly didn't in my time. Or have things changed?"

"Well. Can't complain," Archie had retorted, knowing full well that the evening would set him back several hundred pounds, something he could little afford. Moreover, the sore head with which he would likely awake in the morning would receive scant sympathy from Georgina.

Yet Archie continues to frequent the same leisure centre, clinging to it like a vestige from a happier era. He no longer plays squash, but always swims. Swimming has become for Archie a form of forgetting; forgetting the reassuringly conventional tedium of family life and his job, the fact that he appears to be on a relentless and unending treadmill, condemned to a process of all-too-familiar daily repetition and boredom, worse perhaps than that of a caged hamster. Sinking into the water represents a form of oblivion, a descent into a much more primal way of life. Here, in the depths of the pool, he does not have to talk to, engage with, or compete against anyone at any level. At the end of each swim, Archie feels himself emerging from the pool in an almost Promethean state (he is proud of having developed this metaphor, and has considered – but thus far refrained – sharing it with his fellow pool-goers), as if he were reborn, ready to confront whatever challenges lie ahead.

It is with this image in his mind that Archie has gradually found himself making up more and more excuses to Georgina. Plausible alibis now trip readily off his tongue, but Georgina is rarely impressed: "short-notice breakfast meeting with clients, Georgie, you know how it is;" or, "urgent deadline on the Bartholomew project; an early start and late finish for me today – got to dash, toodle-pip." And perhaps, "surely, Georgie, I mentioned that team bonding dinner we've got tonight; the chaps would be so disappointed if I wasn't there." When he should be at home, he is spending increasing amounts of time at the pool. And if not the leisure centre, then on the streets surrounding it. He is drawn to them, perhaps like the lark to the sky.

It started innocuously enough one night several years ago. As Archie recalls, it had been a tedious black-tie event (luckily he was well used to these by now), a gathering of some arcane legal society for ex-Oxonians held in one of the hotels on Park Lane. Archie had been thoroughly bored, irritated by the underlying current of one-upmanship and dissatisfied by the unoriginal menu. He had excused himself from the particular conversation in which he had been engaged, and briskly exited the building. Yet he had been by no means ready to head home, reluctant to face the mundane remonstrations that would inevitably accompany his return. The night was mild and so the prospect of a walk appealed. After some minutes, he found himself on the Edgware Road.

At night, it was a revelation for Archie; a palate of vibrant life and colour, and about as abrupt a contrast with Moor Park as he could have conceived. There, the only sounds at this time of the evening were the occasional car engine, the intermittent barking of disobedient dogs, perhaps the hum of a lawnmower and, of course, the unendingly regular thrum of the Metropolitan line trains, a distant yet constantly malign presence. Here, on the Edgware Road, by contrast, Archie encountered a veritable pot-pourri, a medley of languages and an intermingling of cultures. As red London buses crawled up the road, their progress punctuated by car horns, police sirens and loud voices, groups milled and melded. Just ten minutes from the pool and here were peoples Archie had never seen in the changing rooms, at least not during the times he visited.

Archie had pressed gamely on, past the groups smoking shisha pipes, others sipping from miniscule cups of coffee; through their greetings and gestures. No one seemed even to notice his attire, black amidst a carnival of colour. By this time, a thirst for further alcohol had settled on him. Archie recalled that there was a large hotel further up the Edgware Road. It was a place that some of his colleagues had made references to, conveniently close to Paddington for visiting clients, or to stay in the event of missed trains home after extended hours in the office. There would undoubtedly be a bar there; somewhere he could comfortably dissolve into anonymity, be just another person looking or hoping for something meaningful while contemplating his whisky, defying time before the inevitable return to normality. On the other hand, if he were lucky, there might even be the chance to strike up a conversation. Surely there would be someone with whom he could engage, who might be a willing recipient of his opinions and grievances; anyone – although preferably a woman – who might show some more interest in him than his wife.

However, Archie never made it to the Hilton that night. With the hotel in sight, a garish green sign bearing the name 'Casanova Night Club' had caught his attention. Archie had paused and found his mind wandering. First, he considered idly what the connection between Giacomo Casanova, citizen of Venice, and the Edgware Road might possibly be. Next, a pulse of resentment seethed. Venice had always been somewhere he had been keen to visit, an almost obligatory stop on the Grand Tour for generations past, a place of history and adventure, but somewhere which had never been on Georgina's agenda. Family holidays tended to take the form of farmhouses in Brittany or gîtes in the Provence. They were rarely pleasurable.

His moment of contemplation had been just long enough for Archie to be assailed by the man guarding the door to the club. The promise of not only drinks, but also a 'floor show with girls' drew him in. At the least, it represented a far cry from his more mundane social programme. The candlelit dinners at the golf club and tedious quiz evenings at his local pub with its semi-rustic interior of replica timber beams, mounted stag's heads and an absurd tartan carpet generally bored him.

And it was indeed a pleasurable time he spent at Casanova's, Archie mentally recounts, pushing open the door to the leisure centre and now humming away again. His memory summons up a descent of red-carpeted stairs and a recollection of the establishment's mirrored walls. Below, in this subterranean cavern of opportunity, were tables spread out around a stage, nubile women parading in heels and golden bikinis and waiters in starched white tuxedos bearing trays of drinks. Archie had taken a seat. Soon, he was joined by a girl (Anima, if his memory serves him correctly), served a glass of his favourite whisky and involved in a pleasant conversation. "Archie. This man – Mr. Casanova from Italy – you say he is called. He sounds *so* interesting. Buy me a drink and tell me more." Few people ever expressed this much enthusiasm when Archie got talking. Later, Anima had to go and perform a belly dance routine on stage, which Archie remembers watching hungrily before he was joined by another girl (Raquel, he believes; later, he got to know all their names). It was all very enjoyable. Before he knew it though, his watch, his wallet and the depths of his conscience reminded him that there were barely minutes before his last train home.

Yet Archie returned, emboldened by his experience. He also ventured further, pacing the streets and constantly seeking the novel. Archie enjoys likening himself to a twenty-first century flâneur. He is rather tickled by this idea, and cares neither that the works of Walter Benjamin are somewhat unfashionable nor that the few to whom he speaks about them ever *fully* appreciate his use of Benjamin's most famous concept. Certainly the girls in Casanova's never did. An explorer, a connoisseur of the street, an emblematic icon of the urban, modern experience; all of this has distinct appeal for Archie. The Edgware Road and its environs certainly could not compare architecturally to the streets of Haussmann's Paris about which Benjamin first wrote, but for Archie this has never mattered; rather it is about the area's possibilities and the potential for something different.

Another memory comes unprompted to Archie's mind at this moment. One evening, he had found himself at a place called Crawford's. It was, he recalled subsequently with some embarrassment, just minutes from the leisure centre, an unfortunate intersection of his daytime and nocturnal existences. There was luckily no overlap of clientele. Crawford's was *very different* to the Casanova Club. White-washed stairs led to a sparsely furnished basement below a shop on Crawford Street. Apart from a small bar discreetly located in the corner, there was little beyond dark leather sofas in the room. But the girls; they were something else. Here, Archie had attempted a conversation with Evelina, the first who had spoken to him. "Tell me more about your home-country, Kyrgyzstan," he had insisted. However, she had been more interested – especially once Archie had bought her a glass of champagne – in removing her small black pants and displaying her immaculately shaven pubic area just inches from Archie's face. It then clicked exactly what this place must be about. Archie, although dissatisfied on many fronts with domestic life, had never seriously contemplated having an affair, let alone engaging the paid services of a woman. He could not summon up the effort, the additional burdens it might impose, the pain of more arguments, accusations and denials.

Yet here was Evelina. She was very pretty and seemed willing. Archie justified it to himself as an experience, a brief moment of intimacy that he realised he would never be able to tell anyone about. In the end, there wasn't much to tell. The whole business was conducted with almost indecent haste, Archie recalls. After, he had felt a distinct sense of anti-climax. And then there had been the journey home to contemplate, yet again.

Now, of course, both Casanova's and Crawford's were shut, and had been for some years. The sorry-looking girls of the night who continue to loiter expectantly on the streets just to the west of the Edgware Road hold no appeal for Archie. Nor do the calling cards displayed brazenly with their extravagant claims and promises in the phone booths up and down the road. He has long since filed his previous indiscretions into a secure place at the back of his mind and subsequently sought to content himself with new adventures, this time of a culinary sort. What a voyage of exploration it remains! On the short stretch of the Edgware Road from Marble Arch to the Hilton, which he considers his territory, Archie encounters within a series of worlds which remain novel to him, still a marked contrast to the Dorking of his childhood, the Oxford of his youth and undoubtedly the environs of his current home. With his excursions regularly taking him into the likes of Fatoush Express, Al Tanoor, Slemani, Melur or Sidi Maarouf, Archie finds himself forming a mental map of the countries whose cuisines are paraded on the street, imagining himself a traveller free from all restraints, perhaps even a lark. Beginning in the west stands Morocco, with its souks, perfect sandy beaches and clustered white houses extending up the hillside; at the eastern perimeter, China's Great Wall represents a natural point of termination. In between, on Archie's metaphorical Silk Road, sits the Middle East, divided in his mind not by politics and arbitrary borders, but by its rivers and mountain ranges, Tigris and Euphrates, Taurus and Elburz. He has never visited any of these countries (and probably never will) but has sampled all of their cuisines and more during his increasingly regular absences from home. It had not taken long for Archie to be able to tell his shwarma from his kofta, his kebab from his farrouj; how the texture of a Lebanese hummus might be ever so slightly different to that of one prepared by an Iraqi; the variations in a Yemeni and Afghani flatbread. The gradual expansion of his waistline provides a fortuitously convenient additional excuse for Archie to proffer to Georgina; his swims are now increasingly *necessary*.

More than the eating though, it is the conversation that he relishes. Archie talks to, and engages with, everyone; the waiters, the customers, sometimes even the chefs. He drinks thirstily the knowledge he gleans, almost desperately, absorbing with willing curiosity the anecdotes imparted by his fellow citizens of the world. Maybe it is a need for intimacy that makes him so eager, although Archie prefers to explain his compulsions from a 'human interest' angle; it is easier this way and just about dovetails with his professional life. During his excursions, he has learned about the seemingly intractable gulf between Sunnis and Shias; heard about war; about refugees and displacement, hope and despair, dreams and nightmares, the legal and the not so legal. Archie had always been good at getting information out of people; it was part of his job, although obviously he never told anyone that he worked as a solicitor, preferring, if at all possible, to shroud himself in a cloak of anonymity.

It is therefore a curious and perhaps unfortunate coincidence, Archie muses, as he is changing that day in the pool, that one of his pending cases at Crispin's relates to a recent incident that occurred on the Edgware Road. A struggle with his red socks (an abominable birthday present from Georgina that he had worn simply to appease her as he left early) temporarily puts him off his stride and halts his humming. Problem righted, he remembers the folders of briefings and other related documents that his assistant had handed him as he was leaving the office yesterday. Fatigue on the journey home and the immediate imposition on his return of an excruciating 'kitchen supper' that Georgina had arranged with some equally awful neighbours had put paid to any attention he may have given them last night. A quick read on the train this morning had to suffice. His papers revealed the usual variety of people whom he would be representing in the coming weeks once he had learned their stories and heard their tales of woe and misadventure; how it was never their fault, how they did not mean to do it, how they didn't realise what the time was, or how much they'd had to drink or that they might ever be found out. As many of his clients were unwitting victims as outright guilty. He'd heard the whole litany of excuses over the years. Archie knows all too well how flawed is humankind.

The case in point that had specifically caught his eye related to an incident that had taken place just minutes from the pool. It would require Archie's appearance in court in the fullness of time. Thinking back, Archie now remembers having heard conversations about the matter over the past weeks in both the changing rooms and the nearby cafes. There had been hints and allegations, wild rumours and much speculation. Now he was going to be involved. In brief, an altercation between some youths had resulted in a fatality; apparently drugs were at the heart of it.

According to the police report, the whole group, victim included, had last been seen congregated together in a place called Perfect Pizza. From where, Archie wondered, did he know that name? Had he eaten there? But surely if he had, he would remember, particularly had the pizzas lived up to the bold claim suggested by the restaurant's name. In the end, Archie had been sufficiently intrigued that he had looked up the details of the restaurant, learning that it was located on the Edgware Road, some minutes north of the Marylebone flyover. This was perhaps why he was not so familiar with it. His explorations of the neighbourhood had usually terminated at the flyover, the bulk of this concrete monstrosity constituting the boundary of Archie's excursions. Beyond this point, the life that characterised the lower part of the road seemed to seep away; there were fewer restaurants with customers spilling onto the streets, more shuttered shops and a long-destitute plot of land that was only now being finally redeveloped. This upper stretch of the street was, Archie had long felt, an older part of London, a potentially darker one, with different histories and secrets.

Now – in the interests of his work, as he justifies it to himself – he has a valid reason to explore further. He would have to pay a visit to

Perfect Pizza. It would provide him with useful context material for the upcoming case, even if it may not hold as much culinary promise as some of his more favoured haunts in the area. He could go after work that day. It would certainly be better than returning home to face the usual frustrations, challenges and criticisms. He cannot recall what events Georgina may have planned, but the idea of a minor rebellion pleases Archie, particularly after their morning altercation. With a plan of action, his clothes and briefcase now in his locker, and the door closed, Archie heads towards the showers and then the pool's water. He starts to hum. Soon, he hopes that he may be almost Promethean again.

MARIUSZ

Mariusz is worried. He frets constantly. The smaller issues nag at him regularly, like an ache that stubbornly refuses to go away, often catching him unaware and unprepared. He has been in England for seven months, yet feels he still does not fully understand the English, their strange manners and curious behaviour. Then there are his other concerns, which relate to money. All he wants to do here is earn enough and return to Poland. Then, he will be able to marry Marta, his childhood sweetheart, and provide her with the life he believes she deserves. He will have hopefully saved sufficient sums to support his parents and younger siblings. Money has been less of an issue recently. Indeed, in the past month, Mariusz has made more than he ever thought possible. But this is the problem. His activities have not been legal. Dark images now form constantly in Mariusz's head. The prospect of arrest, maybe jail, even possible deportation, occupies almost his every waking moment. He thinks of the shame and the ignominy it would bring, worries what his family and his friends may think, whether he would ever be forgiven. Above all, he curses his own stupidity.

On his walk to the swimming pool that morning, Mariusz's mind wanders back to how much has changed during the short time he has been in London. He feels both assimilated and rejected by the city. He constantly marvels at its enormity yet realises how little he really knows about the place and its people. Mariusz had not been naive enough to believe that people in London would all be regularly talking about the

Queen or sipping milky tea from quaint china cups, but nothing had prepared him for the immensity, the unrelenting pulse of the city; its persistent noise and the perennial absence too of a star-filled night sky. The streets, parks, shops and bars of his home in Żary were as familiar to him as his own hands. Almost everywhere he went, he would be recognised and would revel in being in a community of friendly faces. In London, Mariusz observes, most people avoid eye contact and seek generally to shield themselves from any form of involvement with others.

He recalls, with something approaching a grim smile, his initial disappointment on arriving in the city. His flight had left late and Mariusz had dozed off, irritated by the delay and anxious to get there. When he awoke, the plane had just bumped through a bout of turbulence and broken the cloud cover. He was greeted by a leaden-grey sky, the colour of a dirty rag. It felt as if someone had turned off all the lights. Where, Mariusz had wondered, were the River Thames, the Houses of Parliament, the London Eye, all of which he been hoping to see on his descent? Minutes later the plane hit the runway with an abrupt jolt. Fat drops of rain splattered against the windows as the pilot welcomed them to Stansted Airport. Mariusz had immediately turned on his phone and looked again at the details of the place where there he would be staying. From here, he realised, it would take at least another two hours.

As he had sat on the train some while later heading into London, Mariusz remembers the wave of depression that had initially engulfed him. He began to worry that he had made the wrong choice in coming here. Almost no one was talking. Instead, people had their heads pressed into their phones or newspapers. When he stared out of the window, all he saw was a continuum of bleak, flat and empty fields. Such fields existed in Poland too, but their bleakness somehow felt different here, sadder perhaps. He had expected England to be grander, its landscape more imposing. The fields gave way to houses, but it was all so ugly, Mariusz felt. Meanwhile the clouds continued to lour ominously. As he had hit Liverpool Street, Mariusz was confronted with a seething mass of people, mostly wearing suits. The whole place seemed so large and confusing. Buying a ticket for the underground had been a nightmare. Everyone had been so rude and unfriendly.

"Please sir, how do I get a ticket to the Goldhawk Road station?" Mariusz had asked a passer-by.

"Do I look like I work for the underground?" the man had responded. "Find someone who does." Everyone seemed cross and in a rush. Announcements from the PA system constantly blared. He had been able to make out the odd word, most notably "delay."

Mariusz tried again with another person. "Get yourself an Oyster" he was told.

This made no sense at all to him; had he missed something in translation? "An oyster?" he responded, but the man had already walked away.

Finally, a friendly lady – old enough to be his mother – had helped him out, explained that his bank card would let him onto the system and that he would not even need to change train to get to his destination.

Mariusz thanked her and made his way onwards. Entering the underground had, however, felt to him as if he were making a journey into some version of hell. Elbows and briefcases banged into him. A stench of stale sweat mixed with wet leaves pervaded the carriage. Hordes descended and ascended at each station, but the smell did not change. Mariusz remembers feeling relief when the train got as far as Paddington. Not only were there now fewer people, but they had at last emerged into full daylight, the carriages suddenly rumbling above ground. But all Mariusz had seen was concrete everywhere and still none of the famous sights. There was no green and no river. Instead, his vision was occupied with unending rows of terraced houses, relieved only by grey brick estates. Tower blocks loomed as forbiddingly as mountain peaks. Traffic thundered nearby over a huge flyover. There were no sheep at Shepherd's Bush or trees at Wood Lane; just warehouses and storage yards, pick-up depots and multi-storey car parks.

When he had alighted the train at Goldhawk Road, new sounds and smells hit his senses. There was a cacophony of noise; car horns, sirens and more languages being spoken than he had ever heard before. His nose took in an unpleasant combination of petrol fumes and fried food as he continued towards his final destination. There he would be sharing a room with Jacek, a good friend of his brother-in-law, Tomek. It had been Tomek's idea originally that Mariusz should come to London. His sister, Kasia, had recently got married and moved in with Tomek. While there was now one less mouth to feed in the Jankowski household, it meant more work for Mariusz and Paulina, his other sister. Not only did they have their father's rasping cough and increasingly ill health to deal with – he should never have worked in the metal factory for so long – but their younger siblings, Dawid and Pawel, to support. Over the years he had known Tomek, Mariusz had heard him recount many stories about how there was good money to be made in London, way better than could ever be earned in Poland or even over the border in the nearby Czech Republic. Some people, he had learned, were making more than three times what might be possible for doing the same work in Żary. As it happened, a bed had recently become free in the house Jacek currently shared with four other Poles. Tomek had originally been offered the opportunity, but he now had his wife to think of. They wanted to have kids soon too. After several phone calls and family conferences, it was agreed that it would be in everyone's best interests for Mariusz to make his way in London. Later, he would be able to return as the pride of his family, a wealthy man who had seen the world. He would be a role model for his younger brothers; one day, they might follow in his footsteps.

It was these thoughts that had kept him going in those early days, a period he now looks back on almost fondly, as a time of relative innocence. London was always going to be a contrast to Żary. Of course, he missed his home town, its cobbled streets crammed with colourfully painted houses in the centre, the medieval fortifications that still surrounded much of the town, the ever-visible towers of the Sacred Heart Church, and the majestic Green Forest just to the south of the city. Mariusz remembers his continued sense of bewilderment at the sheer *size* of London. He had read somewhere that more than 200 times as many people lived here compared to Żary. Whereas Warsaw (the biggest city Mariusz had encountered prior to London) had had to wait until 1995 to get its first underground line, London had eleven. It would be getting a twelfth soon and this explained the piles of mud and scurrying diggers on the approach into Paddington that he would observe on his now daily ride to Edgware Road underground station. Everywhere Mariusz looks, the city seems to be in constant flux, a state of never-ending renewal, cranes competing for space on the crowded skyline. People in London, it seems, constantly want to build higher, longer, deeper or better. They show little reverence for the past, but, in the pursuit of their dreams, there is money to be made. Buildings need builders, and this is why Mariusz is here.

The people in London, however, never cease to amaze Mariusz. As he looks across at the man in the pool's changing rooms with the silly red socks, Mariusz thinks that he or his wife would be exactly the sort who would reach immediately for their phone and call for a workman every time something goes wrong. Mariusz is astonished by how lazy and free with money many English appear to be. They refuse to paint, plumb or drill; they simply find others who will do it for them. The odd thing though, Mariusz ponders once again, is that the English seem rarely to be at ease with themselves; they are constantly apologetic, finding excuses or justifications for what may have gone wrong or got broken. He has probably heard the word "sorry" more than any other since he has been in London. They also regularly take refuge in conversation about the weather. Indeed, despite having heard much complaining on the part of others, the climate in London does not strike Mariusz as being markedly different from that in Żary. Furthermore, he continues to marvel at how inappropriately people seem to dress for the weather, particularly many of the women. Mariusz's thoughts inevitably turn to Marta. He misses her and looks forward to the day when they can be married. The tattoo he has of her name on his arm (to add to the others he has adorning his torso) acts as a constant reminder of her. He is grateful for the technology that allows him to speak to her regularly. Mariusz makes a point of listening with interest to the events from her day, her stories, offering advice or sympathy where necessary. He has always treated her with respect. He is polite and courteous and remains shocked by how coarse the English seem to be in their attitudes towards women. He has heard their banter on the building sites and in the pub, sometimes even in the pool's changing rooms.

Like so many others, Mariusz has found himself gradually being integrated into London, while simultaneously seeking to retain his connections with Poland. He has learned to recognise and appreciate the city for its diversity, that so many groups seemingly mingle at ease and that his native language is just one of many which he hears spoken every day. No one stands out in London, like they might in Żary if they weren't local, let alone if their skin were a different colour. By contrast, in London, all nationalities are lifted on the tide of the city, which seems to revel in its variety. If he wishes, he can still purchase his beloved kielbasa sausages at the Mleczko Delikatesy on the Uxbridge Road close to his house. But, he is also beginning to develop a taste for bacon sandwiches. He buys Lech beer at the Delikatesy too, but generally drinks something different when he's out. In their shared house, Mariusz is as happy watching Sky Sports as NC+ Poland. He once made the trip to Loftus Road football stadium with a couple of his housemates to see Queen's Park Rangers, their adopted local side. Over 15,000 people had piled into the ground and had cheered both teams raucously. It felt like a world away from the tiny 2,000-seat stadium ground back at home where he would sometimes watch Prominén Żary turn out to play, absurd in their bright yellow strip. It was generally dismal and instantly forgettable third-division stuff. That day in London, the Hoops had won. Among the players on the pitch for the victorious local side had been two Poles – Ariel Borysiuk and Pawel Wszolek – a sight that had cheered him mightily.

It also pleases Mariusz that he can swim in London. This allows him to retain another bond with Żary. The pool near Edgware Road that he has now been going to for some months is a far cry from the Wodnik facility in Żary, but at least it is easy enough for him to get to, both close to where he lives and to the building site where he is currently employed. Even without what he has learned on the job, Mariusz cannot help observe the cracks that have begun to develop at the pool's bottom. He likewise notes the patches of tiles where the grouting has long since disappeared. It continues to confuse him that in a city where there is such an emphasis on renovation, this pool seemingly remains mired in the past. The regulars (he still does not really think of himself as properly being one, and probably never will) love to complain about the state of disrepair, but such behaviour has not translated into any more concrete action as far as he can see. Complaining, he has learned, is another favoured English pastime. In contrast to the leisure centre he uses in London, the Wodnik pool was Żary's pride. He was just a child when the whole complex, with pools, tennis courts and a skate park, had opened. As he thinks back, he can remember his commitment to swimming lessons, then his transition from the kids pool to the main pool. It had felt like a coming of age, being able to swim at last in a proper-sized pool with the men. In later years, he had represented his local school and can remember fondly hurtling through the water, his body forceful like an arrow, the sound of cheering echoing distantly, his family and friends gathered nearby. There had even been talk that he should do trials for the regional team. Swimming had always given him a sense of both unalloyed freedom and power. He could feel in charge of his own destiny. Once he established his rhythm, he was unstoppable. Mariusz swims now in order not just to keep in shape and look good for Marta when he returns; but additionally, to recollect those happy times and to hope that from his time in the pool inspiration for how to resolve his current quandary may emerge.

Finding work in London had not been a problem. This had been one of his initial worries, but Mariusz had soon learned that there was a network – both formal and informal – for obtaining jobs. Word often came of a new project that was starting somewhere, that workers would be required. Sometimes it was a first-come, first-served basis; on other occasions paperwork had to be filled out and contracts to be signed. Mariusz had been determined to do things properly from the outset. He had read up about it. Almost as soon as he had arrived, Mariusz had made sure to get a National Insurance number and open a bank account. It gave him a certain sense of pride to have an English bank card sitting next to the Polish one in his wallet; to be able to check his bank account online and see the pounds building up next to the name 'M Jankowski.' Even if the sums were still small, it pleased him to see the balance getting bigger. He almost wished there were more people with whom he could share his sense of elation and contribution, that he was in England and was making a good, honest living.

At least he had been lucky in finding himself working for Tom Stratton. It was Jerzy, one of his housemates, who had mentioned to Mariusz one evening that he heard on the grapevine that a guy for whom he had done some work in the past was looking to assemble a new team for a major renovation project. Mariusz had warmed to Tom Stratton the first time he had met him. Owner of 'Stratton's, the Master Builder,' he was a self-made man; it was his own business, which he had built up through a combination of hard work, persistence and pragmatism. Unlike many of the English whom Mariusz had met, Mr Stratton did not mince his words.

"I like you Poles – Czechs and Slovaks too, all you Eastern Europeans – you work a darn sight harder than most Brits. And another thing, if Jerzy recommends you, then that's good enough for me," he said when he met Mariusz for the first time.

"Nie ma pracy, nie ma ciasta," Mariusz uttered in response, without thinking.

Stratton laughed. He had heard the old Polish expression, "no work, no cake," before.

Mariusz had impressed Tom Stratton from the outset. "You've shown exactly the sort of attitude I expected, Mariusz boy," he said. The behaviour Mariusz considered to be normal, he soon learned, was in fact far from commonplace. Mariusz would always stand aside to let people pass on the pavement when going to or from the skip or the van. On arriving at someone's house for the first time, he would not think twice about taking off his shoes. It continued to amaze him just how few people did this. In Poland, it was considered a sign of respect. Houses he entered there would almost always have slippers or house shoes available for guests to use. He would always flush the toilet after using it and then wash his hands before returning to the site. He certainly did not expect to be made cups of weak milky tea (which he detested anyway) and would always bring sandwiches from home to eat on site. Mariusz never thought twice about being helpful. Only the other day, he had been returning from Stratton's van empty-handed when he noticed the lady from the house next door struggling with her multiple bags of shopping. He had instantly offered to help and had been rewarded not just with a smile but also the sight of her well-toned figure preceding him to the front door. His balls involuntarily tighten in his swimming trunks as he pictures her once again. Mariusz, however, quickly rejects the thought and tries to replace it with the more wholesome image of his girlfriend.

The job on which he is working is a good one. Mariusz has heard Mr Stratton saying that the work should last a year and maybe longer. A whole house in Little Venice was going to be gutted, its interior replaced, and a basement layer inserted. When Mr Stratton had first told him about the project, Mariusz had not been at all familiar with the area in which he would be working for the foreseeable future. The only Venice he was aware of lay in Italy; not that he has been there, although he's heard it is very romantic. If he worked hard enough then he planned to take Marta there on their honeymoon. She liked the idea of canals and ice cream. He had no real image of what Venice would be like, but he remembers that when he had arrived on the first morning at the site on Blomfield Road in London, his eyes had almost popped out. Mariusz had never seen anything quite like it before. Large, white stucco-fronted houses complacently graced the canal. Sculpted columns such as those he believed adorned ancient temples stood majestically to the sides of imposing black doors. Each was apparently owned by just one family. Mariusz speculated what sort of money would be needed to buy such a property. It was more than he could conceive. What, he wondered, would people do with a house that size; surely it would be hard to find a use for all the rooms? It was certainly bigger than any property he had ever seen in Żary. The more he thought about it, the more Mariusz's mind began to boggle. It made no sense to him why someone who owned such a property would want to rip it apart; to mess with history, and get rid of the mouldings, the wallpaper, almost all the original features.

Still, it was good work and ultimately Mariusz didn't really care if the house would end up looking modern and sterile with its white walls and chrome finishes. He enjoyed the lifting and carrying, the drilling and plastering, the sanding and planing. He liked the variety and odd jobs, especially the occasions when he got to drive the van down the Edgware Road to pick up some parts or paints from the local hardware stores. Sometimes when it was a Friday and Mr Stratton was on site and in particularly buoyant mood, he would suggest that someone grab lunch for the team: "Pizzas on me today boys! You, Mariusz, or Vadim, hop in the van and get down to that Perfect Pizza place. Here's fifty quid. Keep the change, but hop on it now." Mr Stratton was good at doing little things like that, helping to boost morale. When he had initially spoken with his family and friends in Poland, Mariusz had sometimes found that he had to stop himself from sounding as if he were boasting or appearing too pleased with his fortune. Every day, he had believed, his vision of returning home and then taking Marta to Venice was coming a little closer.

As he finishes putting his clothes in the locker at the pool and heads in the direction of the showers, Mariusz worries, once again, about whether his dream won't now be shattered. And all because of something stupid he should never have got involved with. It had started when he had gone for a drink with Benji and Klajdi after work one evening. Mariusz did not know either of them that well, but they were sometimes on site to do work and Mr Stratton in particular always seemed pleased to see them. There was a certain element of coiled aggression in both of them, Mariusz had felt. When they had offered to buy him a beer, Mariusz had thought that to refuse them might cause offence, and so he accepted. After work, Mariusz was normally more content having a swim and then going home for a can or two of drink on the sofa. It wasn't that he didn't like pubs; on the contrary, it was just that he found them very expensive. As he had sat sipping his lager, already calculating how much he would have to spend buying the next round, Mariusz listened to their story. It was hard to follow, not just because of the broken English that they all shared, but also since it seemed that one or other of his companions was constantly out of their seat, picking up their phone and nipping outside to take what appeared to be a series of important calls.

Benji and Klajdi, he had learned, were brothers who had left Tirana several years ago and had settled in London. The brothers complained about Tirana. Benji had called it a shithole, Klajdi the arse-end of nowhere. Both said it was dirty and polluted. Waste, apparently, would often lie uncollected in the street. One of them grumbled about the number of beggars, the other about how hard it was to make money in Albania. London, by contrast, they asserted, was a much better place to make money, if you knew what you were doing. The talk then moved on to girls. Klajdi talked about how beautiful the women were in Albania, olive-skinned with dark eyes and curved figures. Benji told a story about how he had once screwed an English girl, how pale she was and how she had made almost no noise at all in bed, not crying out like the girls back home always did. They had all laughed at this, although Mariusz can recollect – still now – feeling guilty about not admitting to having a girlfriend, yet joining in the chat, as if complicit. As he had returned from the bar with his round of beers, the conversation shifted back to money. One of the brothers observed that the money here was so much better than in Tirana, but then again, beer did not cost almost

£5 for a pint. Mariusz had agreed and, as he settled more into their company, began to explain about having to support his father while providing for his younger siblings too. It was at this stage that Benji had asked Mariusz if he fancied earning some extra money.

Mariusz had not been anticipating the conversation to take this turn, but he listened as Klajdi went on. It was, he explained, very simple. All Mariusz would have to do was deliver a small parcel. He would pick the package up from one of them, take it to someone else and then return with a different package. When they were happy, Mariusz would get his payment, his reward for having completed the delivery. As the brothers put it, there was little more to it than being a postman. Mariusz asked what he would be delivering.

A quick look passed between Benji and Klajdi. "Snow," one of them had said quietly. Mariusz's evident bewilderment must have been obvious to the brothers, for Benji pressed on: "you know, blow, white, snuff, coke."

At last, Mariusz's expression changed. Of course, it must be drugs they were discussing. They weren't his thing and he knew very little about them. Sure, there had been a certain crowd in Żary who had been into smoking and maybe other stuff too, but he had always steered well clear of the whole scene, fearing it might impact on his swimming. He did not like to be out of control. With the look of surprise that must have crossed Mariusz's face, he can recall how Benji had continued to press the point: "everyone is doing white in London these days. The guys in suits. Students. Builders. Even the boss man."

Mariusz's sense of confusion grew. He had not thought of himself as particularly naive or blinkered to the way Londoners might live. Yet if Benji and Klajdi were to be believed, then drug-taking was apparently as much part of the city's culture as drinking. Nonetheless, his caution prevailed and Mariusz had pressed the brothers, asking them why they wanted him to do the work, why they did not do it themselves. Klajdi explained in a few scrambled sentences which Mariusz did not fully understand something to do with anonymity and chains, degrees of separation. Benji perhaps had a better gauge of Mariusz and said that it was because everyone said he was a hard worker and was very trustworthy, particularly Mr Stratton. Mariusz still had his doubts, but then asked just how much money it might – theoretically – be possible to earn from helping them. When one of them mentioned the figure, Mariusz can recall almost falling off his seat in the pub; *that much*, just for delivering one package?

The following day, after a mostly sleepless night of intense deliberation, his thoughts having pulled him in both directions, Mariusz had sought out Benji on the site. If it was as easy a task as they had claimed, with his role being just that of intermediary rather than dealer, he reasoned that he might soon be a richer man and retain an almost clear conscience. His family would not ever need to know the source of his earnings and perhaps he would be able to return home sooner than originally planned. He and Marta could maybe have a grander honeymoon too. Benji shook his hand, took his phone number and told him to expect a call. Two days later, at the weekend, Mariusz had received a text. It was from Benji, asking him if he could be at a car park in Acton within the next hour. Mariusz can recall the chill of nervousness yet also perhaps excitement – a little like the sensation before diving into the pool at the start of a swim meet – that had travelled down his spine and then into his gut as he journeyed on the bus. Klajdi was there waiting. He passed Mariusz a brown A5 envelope and gave him an address that he could type into his phone. All he was told to do was knock on the door. He would be expected. He should just hand over the package and then receive a similar one in return. Mariusz was assured that there would be no problems. Klajdi had added, perhaps somewhat darkly, that if there were, then they would be dealt with; he was not to worry. Fifteen minutes later Mariusz had found himself in a block of flats on the White City Estate. His knock had been answered by a man in a shiny new tracksuit with a vacant-eyed look of indifference. Quarter of an hour after that, Mariusz was back at the car park, handing over the package he had received. Klajdi just nodded, shook Mariusz by the hand and then pressed some notes into his palm. Back at home Mariusz had begun to wonder whether he had dreamed the whole thing. It was the brevity of the experience, the ease of the task and the sudden appearance of money. On Monday, Mariusz had paid the money into his bank account and transferred it to his family in Poland, leaving aside enough just to buy a new pair of swimming goggles, the same pair he is wearing today, although they now feel tainted and somehow wrong. At the time, however, he can remember his family's elation when he Skyped them that evening.

"Mariusz, our golden boy! How are you? How is England? Have you seen the Queen (His Dad always made the same terrible joke)? How is the weather?"

"All is well, Tati. The weather is getting warmer. And, no, I have not seen the Queen yet."

"Soon Mariusz, you will, particularly since you are doing so well in England. You are making us all so proud with the money you are earning. Your brothers are desperate to go there too. Aren't you kids?" Mariusz could see them nodding eagerly.

"Yes, I am working hard. I got some extra money too, for all the jobs I am doing." It was only a small lie, but it had been worth it, just to see the expressions on their faces.

"Keep it up my son, keep it up. You remember boy, that's what I said to you when I used to take you to those swimming events. It's a race son, and you're winning."

"Yes, Tati." By now Mariusz was keen for the call to be over. "Lots of love, I'll call you soon. Bye!"

The second and third deliveries he made for the brothers were similarly uneventful, one comprising a trip to a flat in Notting Hill, another to an ugly council block on the Kensal Road, the roar of the nearby Westway ever-present. It was the fourth occasion, however, that had upset Mariusz. The address he'd been given was for a building called Kennet House. When Mariusz had looked up its location, he realised it was on Church Street, just off the Edgware Road and remarkably close not just to the builders' merchants he might visit during the day, but also to the pool. He had climbed six flights of stairs in the depressing tower block (the lift, of course, was broken) and was looking forward to when this job would be over, regretting only that the leisure centre would probably be shutting and so he could not visit after. He had pressed the buzzer. Moments later, the door opened a crack.

"What?" The voice sounded young and very nervous.

"I have your delivery," Mariusz responded. This was the answer he had been instructed by Benji and Klajdi to give.

"You've got the stuff?" There was clear desperation in the tone, but a hint of hostility too. The door opened further and Mariusz could see that the occupant of the flat was not only very young, but clearly out of his depth, uncomfortably sweating and twitching fretfully.

"Yes."

"Well, hand it over – and quick." The boy scanned the corridor feverishly for signs of movement.

"Money first."

A shaking hand passed over an envelope to Mariusz. He returned the gesture. There was no eye contact, no other exchange. The door slammed shut. Before Mariusz had turned, he could hear the chain being pulled roughly across.

During his descent the thought had suddenly struck Mariusz that the boy would probably have been almost the same age as his brother Dawid. At this moment, Dawid would likely be finishing his homework, or mucking about on his phone, while his parents would be sitting in front of the television set in the small but comfortable house they had always owned in Żary. It was beyond his sphere of reference to imagine Dawid being involved in anything as sordid or as potentially terrifying as a transaction concerning illegal drugs. Mariusz can recall how feelings of guilt and apprehension had washed over him. Although it was out of character, he left the tower block and walked straight into the pub that lay almost opposite, a miserable-looking building named the Lord High Admiral. Other than the curious stares from the locals, he has no recollection of the place, just how the sour and metallic taste of the vodka he had downed immediately had burned his throat. He had dry-retched as he left the premises. The sensation almost repeats itself as he stands in the pool's showers that morning. At the time, Mariusz told himself that this would be the last instance he would work for the brothers.

Mariusz did not mention anything that evening, when he had met Klajdi and handed over the money-stuffed envelope he had received from the boy in the flat. The problems, however, had begun two days later. When he had arrived at work, there was none of the usual chatter about football or what tasks were pending and which supplies might be needed. Instead, all the conversation had seemed to centre on stories of a murder that had occurred nearby the previous night. No one quite knew the facts and much of the debate seemed to be just speculation, but the words "teenagers," "local" and "drugs" cropped up with regularity. Mariusz had not contributed much to the topic, pretending to busy himself with a complex task, but he had already begun to join the dots in his head and form an ugly conclusion. Not long after that someone had mentioned that Mariusz was looking rather pale. Someone else had asked him whether he was feeling OK. He mumbled the first thing that came to his mind, a comment about having had a dodgy pizza the night before. Mariusz had only hoped that his lie was convincing enough to be believed. He had asked Mr Stratton – who seemed in a foul mood that morning – whether he could have the day off, since he was feeling unwell. Mariusz was told that he could, but that he would obviously not get paid. Money was the least of his worries.

Ever since, Mariusz has continued to fret. His problem is compounded by the fact that he feels there is no one with whom he can discuss his range of feelings, his fears and his uncertainties. He knows that there is no way in which he could broach the topic with his family – they would be shocked, as would Marta. Mariusz doubts whether his flatmates would be sympathetic and he does not trust anyone on the building site. He is certainly reluctant to bring the subject up with the Albanians. He is not surprised that he has heard nothing from them since his last assignment. Mariusz has begun to realise that this is his gruesome secret, and that he will have to live with it. A series of thoughts continue to play and then replay through his mind. There is no way he can be sure that he was involved in the chain of events that recently played out, that it was the drugs *he* delivered that resulted in someone dying. He does not know whether any of the other people who had been present at the murder scene might confess to where they had obtained the drugs. Mariusz knows nothing about English law, whether he might be considered an accessory to murder. Would he, in turn, mention Benji and Klajdi, and what might be the consequences of so doing? Mariusz is nervous every time he hears a police siren. He feels that the police stations he passes on the Edgware Road after leaving the pool and in Shepherd's Bush, opposite the Mleczko Delikatesy on his way home, are silently mocking him, haunting him and reminding him of his terrible error.

As he exits from the shower that morning, the doubts and questions continue to whir through Mariusz's brain. The swim, he hopes, will help take his mind off things. He is looking forward to the plunge, the immersion, the white noise, the repetitive motion of the strokes, the thoughts of competition and success. At least much of the talk at the building site has now moved onto other things. Before diving into the water, Mariusz consoles himself with the thought that no one at the building site (other than the now-absent Benji and Klajdi) – or for that matter the pool – either knows of or suspects the role he may have played in recent events. The police have not come for him yet, and now the water beckons.

LEON

Leon is angry. He is angry about many things – about the injustice, the stupidity and other people's lack of understanding. There is a numbness too. The whole thing still seems unreal, at times almost dream-like. He wishes that none of it had ever happened, or that it has been happening to someone else. But it isn't. Instead, there is a constant reconstruction in his mind of what took place, also how and why it did. Leon has no clear answers. None of it makes any sense. More than anything, he feels the absurdity of the situation, its utter incomprehensibility. Leon stares around the pool's changing room with open hostility. He wonders whether anyone here has ever known true tragedy; how they could possibly understand what it feels like for your first-born child to have died so abruptly, his life curtailed at the age of seventeen, his potential unfulfilled.

The sound of the abrupt knocking on his front door that fateful evening eighteen days ago still feels as fresh to Leon as if it had just happened. It was the moment when his existence lost all bearing, when his previous hopes and plans – and more than that, his assumptions – were cruelly undermined, his very sense of purpose undone. At the time, Leon had been asleep. The harsh and insistent noise had forced him to rise reluctantly from bed. Pulling on his dressing gown crossly, he had wondered who could be calling at this hour. Surely it would have to be important or the caller would have already given up. By the time he had reached the bottom of the stairs Joy had arrived as well, emerging from the bathroom. She was similarly bewildered. Both had exchanged a glance of surprise and perhaps slight fear before Leon opened the door. Fortunately, the noise had not awoken the younger children, while Samuel was probably out and about somewhere, doing his own thing. The sight of two policemen on their doorstep was not what they had been expecting. No one ever expects or prepares you for this, Leon would think back later, time and again. Their combined bulk seemed to fill the doorway, their crisp uniforms a stark contrast to the slightly dishevelled outfits of Leon and his wife. Their expressions were impassive. "Mr and Mrs Campbell?" the older of the two officers had asked. Leon had simply nodded. His brain had still not fully clicked into gear.

"It's about your son," the policeman continued.

"What's he done?" Joy asked.

"May we come in?"

Leon had then started to develop the first dark inklings about the seriousness of the matter. A sinking, sickening feeling began to wash through his stomach. At the same time, a range of thoughts were crowding his mind, conflicting and not making sense. Joy held open the door and the policemen had walked in. Their discomfort was evident, their presence incongruous. Static tension hung in the air. There seemed to be a mutual feeling that whatever needed to be said should be, as soon as possible, the whole matter concluded quickly and with minimal fuss. All four had remained awkwardly standing, an offer or decision to sit down perhaps being an indication that the event might need to be prolonged more than strictly necessary.

"I think you ought to sit down," one of the officers had said.

Leon and Joy exchanged another look, one of further incomprehension, but which contained a slowly dawning realisation. A bubble of fear began to rise within Leon as they perched uncomfortably on the edge of their small sofa.

"Are you the parents of Samuel Brandon Campbell?" were the next words uttered by the policeman.

By this stage, neither Leon nor his wife could force any words from their mouths. Both had nodded, simply disbelieving.

"We're very sorry to inform you," the older officer had started. He paused, cleared his throat. "There is no easy way for us to say this." Another pause, and then in a rush, "Samuel Campbell was involved in a fatal incident at 10.14pm this evening."

Nothing would ever be the same for Leon after those words had been uttered. Everything had unravelled. There was a time before, when the presence of Samuel was a given for Leon – something taken for granted and never questioned – even if they had not always got on, as had increasingly been the case recently. Now, there is the time after, a vast and unending plain where there would never be a further moment Leon would spend with his son. Leon is only just beginning to realise that Samuel will never have another birthday to celebrate; there will be no graduation, first job or pay cheque; no girlfriend, marriage or children – there will simply be nothing at all. More than anything, Leon feels an overwhelming sense of guilt, both for things said and unsaid, done and not done. Like a video on constant loop, Leon finds himself going over the same questions time and again. Had it somehow been his fault that Samuel had died; had he not spent enough time with his son; had he been a poor role model in some fashion? And, more than anything, why did Samuel have to die so young, before his own father, thereby subverting the natural order of existence?

The life of the Campbells had not been an easy one. Leon's father had arrived in the UK in 1962, some years after the initial Windrush generation, but at a time when attitudes towards West Indians were still characterised by a combination of ignorance and prejudice. Leon had become familiar with all the stories over the years, particularly those about how London had offered a prospect of romance to the likes of his Dad, but how this expectation had rapidly transformed into disenchantment. Sure, there was work to be had, and good money too, but it had come at a cost. The conditions in which his family had first lived were blighted thoroughly by poverty. The legacy of the War and the damage it wrought had never left the parts of Ladbroke Grove and Westbourne Park where much of the Trinidadian community chose to settle. They had all looked out for each other, welcoming newcomers into the fold; the church and the few shops selling imported goods providing natural focal points. Yet there had been the weather to endure, the endless days of grey skies, the absence of a sun which they had taken for granted in Port of Spain. Leon heard the tale countless times of how his Dad thought he was dying when he arrived in England and breathed out the harsh London air on his first winter's morning – "what is this smoke coming out of my mouth?!" By the time Leon came into the world, his parents had at least begun to accept the weather, even if they would never fully get used to it. The racism though was something different. As a child, Leon can easily bring to mind how a current of violence rumbled perpetually below the surface of the streets where he walked and played. Regularly it would rise up, and openly abusive language or worse would be thrown at him and his friends. Their difference was something unavoidable and inescapable.

When Samuel was born, it had been the abiding hope of Leon and Joy that they would be able to provide him with a better life and greater prospects than either of them had experienced when growing up. They had both hoped that *his future* would hold huge promise; further, that Samuel would have multiple opportunities, in a more tolerant and less judgemental world. Leon slams his fist into his sports bag as he realises once again that there will be no future for Samuel, that his life has been curtailed all too abruptly. He takes a deep breath, tells himself to calm down, that it will be all right in the end. Except it won't. He hopes no one in the changing rooms has spotted his outburst, but doesn't really care if they have. He is beyond being concerned about such matters.

The unending sense of despair engulfing Leon contrasts cruelly with the optimism he had felt when Samuel was born. Their choice of name had been simple, for this was what Leon's father was called, and their son tangible proof of the continuation of the Campbell family line. His and Joy's pride had been immense. Samuel would embody their expectations, go on to do great things. For a moment Leon pauses in his melancholy thoughts and, as he continues to get undressed, casts his mind back to the better times he and Samuel spent together. He recollects the holiday they had saved up for and all taken to Trinidad when Samuel would have been four, the year before his twin sisters had been born. Leon recalls the innocent, pure joy of watching his boy run free in the endless white sand of Maracas Bay and paddling in its warm waters near to where his own parents had decided to settle once his father had retired. He can visualise with perfect clarity the family portrait, the moment his father had held his first-born grandchild and smiled widely.

Before Leon can dwell too long on the brutal fact that *he* will never get to hold Samuel's child, his reminiscences move on again. Samuel had always adored sport of all kinds; he was a natural. Leon thinks now about the countless games of football they used to play together, kicking a ball around the park pretty much whenever Leon was not driving trains. Later, as Samuel got older, Leon would try to watch him play as regularly as possible. He had captained his primary school side as well as playing for a local sports club. Leon pictures the bright floodlights of the five-a-side pitches under the Westway where he would often stand watching Samuel.

"Come on son," he would cheer from the sidelines, "you can do it!"

He remembers his elation at watching Samuel score the winning goal in the youth cup final, punching his fist in the air at the vital shot, "yes!"

And also hugging Samuel after the final whistle. "You were the best, son! I'm so proud of you. The team wouldn't have won the match without you."

"Thanks Dad," was Samuel's modest response, "I'm glad you came to watch. It meant a lot to me."

"I love you son."

"Love you too Dad."

On free weekends when Leon was not working and they could afford it, he would take Samuel to the real thing, a trip to Loftus Road to watch Queen's Park Rangers, their side. As a young boy, Samuel would always wear his replica Rangers strip, dreaming that one day he might be centre-forward for the Hoops, potentially even captaining them in a Wembley final. Music was another bond between them. As a child, Samuel had always been fascinated by Leon's record collection, which he had painstakingly built up over the years, vinyl being one of his few extravagances. Leon evokes fondly how Samuel would dance to everything, from the Supremes to Public Enemy and Chaka Khan to the UMCs. Carnival weekend was always a special moment for the whole family, a time when they would all dress up, watch the floats, the dancing, the colour. They shared in the vibrancy and unbridled enthusiasm that defined the whole event.

Yes, those were good times, thinks Leon. Fathering was undoubtedly one of the best things he had ever done, perhaps the best, now everything else has been thrown starkly into perspective. But, Leon is forced to ask himself once again, how did it all go wrong? He had always considered himself to be a good parent, providing for and supporting Samuel wherever possible, offering advice yet not seeking to interfere excessively in his son's life. They had encouraged his interest in sport and made churchgoing a regular activity since both he and Joy had felt that figures from within these communities would serve as additional strong role models for Samuel. Here, there would be people Samuel would look up to and could talk with, when the presence and perceived meddling of his parents might be just too awkward. They had felt that they were doing a good job.

It was only when Samuel got older that things had started to change. Leon dates it to when his son turned sixteen and started a course in IT at the local college instead of staying on at school. As soon as he had started there, Samuel began to shed his former ties, almost as if he were deliberately deciding to embark on a new way of life. Initially, they noticed that Samuel seemed to have abandoned the majority of his former schoolmates. Leon had felt at the time that this was perhaps understandable, since Samuel would obviously be keen to integrate himself among a new circle of friends. There were only so many hours in the day and, clearly, he was growing up, developing new connections and interests. However, soon other parts of the fabric of Samuel's previous existence began to unravel too. Almost overnight, he announced that he no longer wanted to play football for his club. No explanation was proffered other than he had got bored with it. They decided to let this pass; after all, Samuel was effectively an adult now and they could not force him to participate at the club if he did not want to. When Samuel refused to join his parents and sisters at church on Sunday mornings, the arguments became fiercer, but again, there was little either Leon or Joy could do, even if it did upset them. What made it worse was that Samuel appeared not even to *care* what impact his behaviour was wreaking upon his family.

The distance between Leon and Samuel at this time was widening, gradually, but nonetheless inevitably. It was less a feeling of enmity, but simply that they were operating in alternative spheres with different priorities, now rarely overlapping. In a reversal of the roles they had occupied when they were younger, Leon had increasingly begun to seek approbation or at least recognition from Samuel; yet it was rarely granted. Leon constantly tried to reach out to Samuel, hoping to bring him closer or perhaps just establish some common ground between them.

"You want to go to see the Hoops play this weekend Samuel?"

"Nah Dad. Football don't interest me all that much."

"What about a trip to the Jazz Cafe then son? They've got some good acts coming up next month."

"Maybe. But I'm kinda busy with other things. Will let you know."

Sometimes Leon would text Samuel when his shift ended at Edgware Road Station to see if he were around and wanted to meet up, perhaps for a coffee or even a beer. His messages were almost never answered.

On the increasingly rare occasions when Leon did see his son at home, there were often needless arguments and pointless fights. Samuel would typically refuse to answer either his or Joy's questions, object to doing chores around the house, fail to look out for his younger sisters and so on. Samuel would rarely get annoyed. Rather, his tactic was one of simply retreating into himself, at the same time growing further apart from his parents. More and more, Samuel would choose to be elsewhere; often at friends' houses or simply "out," an explanation which seemed to cover almost everything. Sometimes he would even spend the night elsewhere. If Leon and Joy were lucky, he might send a text explaining his whereabouts. But not always.

Leon and Joy had, of course, speculated on what might be the matter. They wondered whether perhaps Samuel might have a girlfriend. But he gave no indication that this was the case. Even if he did, they reasoned, surely Samuel would be more content, not so surly and despondent. They considered too the possibility of alcohol or drugs. Samuel had never historically shown any significant interest in either – "that sort of thing is for losers," he would say – preferring to focus on sport and his studies. When Leon did encounter Samuel at home, neither his breath nor his clothes smelt of drink or smoke. Meanwhile, Joy's regular searches of his room for potentially incriminating evidence were futile, since none was forthcoming. After many discussions, often covering the same topics, the same lines of debate rehearsed and repeated time and again, Leon and Joy reluctantly reached the conclusion that Samuel was simply going through a difficult phase, something common to many teenagers. Leon recalls the arguments he had had with his own parents. There were rows over him not being committed to studying, or that he was spending too much time listening to music. All Samuel was doing – just as Leon had – was rebelling, trying at the same time to define his own identity.

As his fist tightens again, Leon thinks uselessly that perhaps he and Joy should have paid better attention to what Samuel was doing, asked him more questions, not backed off, but rather got more involved. What makes it worse is that Leon can't even remember when he last saw Samuel or precisely what his final words to his son may have been;

even whether they parted on good terms or bad. He tries desperately once again to reconstruct the past, but fails. Leon had been working early shifts in the week of Samuel's death and so had not seen him in the mornings, already on the trains when Samuel might have surfaced. He is pretty sure that Samuel hadn't put in an appearance in the evenings of that week. When Leon consults his phone – as he does now, once again, in the pool's changing room – he finds that the saved messages he has from Samuel are sparse in quantity and mostly just a word or two long – "maybe", "later" or "yeah, soon" – especially the most recent ones. So much is unanswered, unsaid. Leon's guilt and his anger are compounded by the fact that he wishes he'd told Samuel more regularly that he loved him – for, despite everything, his underlying affection for and faith in his son had been utterly unwavering, never in doubt. He wonders for the umpteenth time when he last uttered those momentous words; similarly whether he had ever heard Samuel repeat the same expression back to him.

Almost nothing makes sense to Leon. If struggling to recall his last moments with Samuel is difficult, then piecing together accurately what happened in the time immediately after his death is even harder. It all seemed to go by in so much of a blur that Leon barely had time to register any of it. There were so many arrangements to make, forms to sign, people to inform. Everybody, it seemed, wanted to meet Leon, often to shake his hand and offer condolences; on other occasions to ask him questions: the police, the principal of Samuel's college, well-meaning neighbours, friends of Samuel's and more. They came, they went, they returned (throughout, the prying journalists were rebuffed).

It seemed like there was rarely a moment of peace in the Campbell household; certainly never a time to grieve properly and process what actually had happened. In the evenings, Leon was generally so weak with exhaustion that all he could do was drag himself to bed. There, his sleep would be deep and empty, the loss of Samuel yet fully to catch up with him. Later there was the funeral. It was a large affair at their local church, a celebration of Samuel's life, and, at the same time, a recognition of its unfortunately abrupt conclusion. The wake had followed, condolences were offered, anecdotes reminisced over and much rum drunk.

Then it was all over. Yet life would never return to normal. Leon recalls the evening of the day following the funeral, when all the distant relatives and family friends had gone. It was just him, Joy and their daughters. They had sat around the dining table eating Joy's special saltfish stew. Nobody said a word. The sound of the clock ticking was the only noise. It filled the kitchen, which seemed both larger and emptier than it had ever done before. The minutes passed. No one appeared to be eating. Leon could see that his daughters kept glancing towards the seat where Samuel would have sat, not that all five of them had been around the table for a long time. Joy was doing it too. Then her phone beeped on the counter, the sound of a message arriving. "Maybe it's…," she began, before trailing off, her voice just about not breaking. Silence returned. A minute later Leon got up wordlessly. He took his plate to the bin, shoved the contents in and then dropped it in the sink, before striding out of the room. As he climbed up the stairs he could hear tears. Later that night, he had held Joy tightly in bed.

They were both shaking uncontrollably, enveloped in grief. Words were not necessary.

Leon had thought it might become easier after this moment. Instead it became much harder. Being together heightened their sense of loss. Samuel's absence was a fact that neither of them could mention, but equally could not ignore. Sharing meals was no longer possible for Leon. It constituted for him both a recognition and an acceptance of their diminished family. Rather than drawing closer, Leon found himself moving further apart. Worse than that, Leon began to resent Joy. Where she found consolation in religion, he derived none. Leon did not need the vicar to tell him that the world was imperfect, that its ways were not ordered and mechanical, but random; this he knew full well. Samuel was the victim of an unfortunate accident. He had found himself out of his depth, with a group of people he barely knew, doing something he didn't fully comprehend and in the wrong place at the wrong time. God might be familiar with loss and grief – that's what Joy told him – but this phrase felt empty and meant little to Leon. It certainly didn't assuage his suffering. He had lost Samuel and his faith too. More than that, as a result, many of the old assumptions – and not just these, but also the intimacies – that he and Joy formerly shared had now weakened. It no longer felt as if they were on the same side. Their sorrows were separate and their individual grieving increasingly irreconcilable.

"I'm taking our daughters to stay with my sister for a while. It will be for the best," Joy had announced to Leon one morning. He had not been surprised and did not object very forcefully. Maybe it would be for the best, he felt. Time apart from each other may allow them to come better to terms with their loss, their grieving, and their ineluctably altered reality. His family absent, all Leon feels he has now is the Underground and the pool. Driving trains and swimming have become the focal points of his existence, constants in a world where nearly all of his previous assumptions have been undermined. Leon knows he should call Joy and speak to his remaining children, but he has barely picked up the phone. Missed calls and unanswered messages blink at him from his handset. He chooses mostly to ignore them and has even considered throwing his phone away, disposing of this remnant from his previous life, and starting again with a new number. Leon is rarely at home now and prefers it that way. The sound of the ticking clock reinforces the emptiness of the place. The TV and the radio have stayed off, their news rarely positive. He cannot face opening the growing pile of post. Even washing the dishes or his clothes constitutes a major undertaking. There are still traces of Samuel everywhere around the house, yet he is nowhere, and never to return.

Leon likes driving trains. He has done it for almost as long as he can remember. It is thirty-two years now, he calculates. He remembers applying for the job at the suggestion of his father, who had done the same thing before moving back to the Caribbean to retire. At the time, the Underground was one of the few places where it made no difference what colour Leon's skin was, nor how old he might be or what sort of educational background he had. On the job, everyone just takes their train around the Circle Line, time and again. You might be your own boss, alone in your cabin, but there is no scope for deviation.

Much of the time he switches off, content with the rhythm of the train on the tracks, the repetitive announcements, the familiar processes of acceleration and deceleration, opening and closing doors. There is the darkness of the below-surface stations, but equally the beautiful contrast of the natural light, emerging west out of Paddington, away from the sooty tunnels and into the fresh air. Leon never gets bored with it. He particularly loves sunrise, the city alive with possibilities at the start of a new day. At night, London extends, the lights from countless houses spread out around him as he travels onwards. From his position at the front of the train, Leon sees countless snapshots of other people's lives. He observes the young and the old, the happy and sad; couples kissing, fighting and making up. There are the aggressive commuters, jostling for prime spots on the platform; the tourists, confused yet excited to be in an unfamiliar city, and many others too, even sometimes faces Leon recognises from the leisure centre. He enjoys watching all these scenes. They are like stills from never-to-be-repeated films, generally forgotten, but occasionally remembered. Almost as soon as one disappears, another replaces it. Each passes him by. He is powerless to alter their preordained course of action.

Over the years, there is little he hasn't seen. Leon has been fortunate though never to have witnessed a suicide, or 'one-under' as the drivers tend to call it. He has heard the stories and the sense of sheer surprise and shock experienced when witnessing such an occurrence. Afterwards, some drivers never work again, being too overcome by what they saw and confronted with their inability to have prevented it. Other drivers have told that it can be as bad being in the train behind, knowing that if only circumstances had been slightly different, then they may have been the one brought face-to-face with death. Irritation courses through Leon once more as he remembers how only yesterday another driver with whom he was on nodding terms had come up to him on the platform as they were changing shifts.

The news of Samuel had somehow reached him. He had been meant well, of course. "I know what you're going through," he said, as he put his hand on Leon's shoulder. "Last year I witnessed a one-under," he continued. "It was difficult, but I got over it. Life has moved on. You know what I mean?"

In the past, Leon might too have offered similar well-meaning but unintentionally insensitive words of condolence to a distraught colleague. But now he is starkly aware how shallow such utterances are. Leon now realises that it is *never true*, that another can know what he may be feeling. The depths of his personal pain, loss and irreconcilability are still unknown even to him. He feels he is far from plumbing their deepest levels. All that he is sure of is that Samuel is lost and irreplaceable.

Leon's mind is constantly filled with such thoughts. He has no answers to his many unsolved questions about Samuel and how things could have been different. But Leon still hopes that he may eventually arrive at some, thereby helping to lift his increasingly heavy veil of frustration and despondency. At least the isolation of his driver's cabin and the depths of the pool offer him ample time to think. Leon knows he needs this. Moreover, it is a lot easier than having to talk to other people. The suggestion of counselling was made by some well-intentioned visitor in the days after Samuel's death, but Leon had steadfastly refused it. To have accepted would – as Leon sees it – have been an admission of defeat, an acknowledgement of his inability to work things through by himself. Furthermore, Leon has barely seen his friends since the funeral. This is his choice. The initial few times they did meet in the immediate aftermath, it was always awkward. They would either attempt to tread gingerly around the topic of Samuel, the unfinished sentences hanging in the air and then trailing away into silence; or, they would simply act as if nothing had happened, chatting away instead about the football or some musician who would soon be performing in town.

Like the Underground, the swimming pool constitutes an alternative sphere of reality for Leon. Every day he walks from the pool to Edgware Road Station, or does the journey the opposite way. Sometimes he swims both before and after his shift, the relative freedom of the water and its blue depths providing a contrast to the mostly black confinement of his underground carriage. Yet both the water and the tracks share much in common too; it is the order, the rhythm and the repetitive process that appeal to him. Leon has swum almost all his life. When he was a kid, his parents would take him to the same leisure centre. There he had made his first tentative movements in the water, gradually abandoning his armbands over time and moving unaided. Since then, swimming has become second nature to Leon. Now, he swims with hard and powerful strokes, pounding under the water from end to end. He never counts the number of lengths, simply swimming mechanically until he is drained and can do no more. The water acts as a form of anaesthesia for the unyielding pain Leon feels.

Although his shifts on the Underground vary, Leon has been coming to the pool for sufficiently long that he recognises most of the faces in the changing room, regardless of the time of day he visits. They are as varied a bunch as are his driver colleagues. Background, age and race make no difference. The water is a great leveller. Most of the people keep to themselves, content in their own routine; their anonymity too. There are always one or two who irritate Leon, such as the man nearby. His plummy tones interrupt Leon's thoughts for a moment. Leon hears that he is telling one of the older guys that some young lad has stolen his locker. There is barely a pause in his unrelenting chatter before Leon notices that he has started on another, seemingly unrelated topic to a different person; this time something to do with some composer that Leon has never heard of. At least he's not talking to Leon and Leon won't have to share a lane with him. Whenever possible, Leon chooses the lane allocated to fast swimmers (the man who likes the sound of his own voice, Leon knows, prefers the medium lane). In *his* lane are people like the young tattooed Eastern European guy Leon now spots on the other side of the changing room. On a few occasions they have spoken briefly about football, especially since Leon learned that they both support Queen's Park Rangers. Looking in his direction, Leon nods curtly at him.

He does not feel in the mood for talking this morning. Leon had slept badly. The same chain of thoughts continued to play unceasingly in his mind throughout the night. He would have had a drink to ease the pain, but the rules don't allow it if he is driving the following day. It might not have made any difference to his mood though. Leon feels perpetually tired, weakened by the burden he carries. He is unsure when – or whether at all – this feeling will lift. The court case where Samuel's murderer will be tried is still weeks away. This may result in some justice being done, thinks Leon, but it will never bring Samuel back. Life will have to go on without him. After his swim, there is his seven-hour shift on the trains. Then he may return to the leisure centre, or perhaps just sit in a nearby cafe staring into space as Leon has found himself doing increasingly recently, the minutes ticking away until it is time eventually to return home. He knows he should call Joy later. There are also bills to be paid, emails to be answered and a seemingly endless list of other things to be done. Now, all Leon wants to think about is the prospect of the water, the opportunity for it to wash away some of his anger. He slams his locker shut and strides towards the pool. Leon knows there is a long day ahead of him.

TONY

Tony is making plans. Top of his list when he lands is to go for a swim. He has slept badly, his body aches and he feels stiff all over. The novelty of flying overnight has long since left him. Stretching, he imagines the sensation of plunging into the pool, and how its waters will cleanse him. Then, he will be ready for anything. As he looks out of the plane's window, Tony feels his optimism renewed. Dawn is breaking, the sky beginning to fill with light. Pale gold streaks appear among the frosty clouds. London is laid out before him in all its glory. There is the sight of the Thames, a vital artery running between the landmarks he knows so well. Past his eyes goes St Paul's, next the London Eye and the Houses of Parliament, then the BT Tower. Regent's Park appears, followed soon after by Hyde Park. However familiar, the view moves him every time, stirring his emotions. It signals arrival. He is coming home, to his city, where his roots lie.

The sun glints from the buildings as the plane makes its final approach. The landmarks give way to suburban sprawl. Yet everything Tony sees looks so still and quiet, almost undisturbed. The day is just beginning. Only a smattering of cars is out on the road. Most people are probably still asleep or maybe now starting to wake. The brief glimpse of a lone milk float out on its round seems almost incongruous, like a vestige from another era. Tony continues to peer out of the window of the rapidly descending plane. Down it goes, gradually slowing; down a bit further; and then, thud. The wheels hit the tarmac hard. With the jolt, Tony is forced back into reality. By instinct, he reaches immediately for his mobile and turns it on, berating himself for doing so at the same time. The temporary bliss of being uncontactable is over.

As soon as he has a signal, Tony checks what has been happening in the financial markets in Asia overnight, then briefly his emails. "Shit! Fucking shit," he swears, a little too loudly, since the passenger in the seat next to him gives him a curious look. Things had been looking bad when he had left New York. He sees now that his firm has lost more money during the time it has taken for his plane to cross the Atlantic. By the looks of it, additional clients might be redeeming their money from the fund he manages. At the least, there will be calls to make and the offer of placatory meetings or lunches. Tony feels a sense of dread weighing heavily upon him. Soon, he will probably need to be on a plane again; it is all part of the never-ending process of having to keep people happy.

Not for the first time, Tony appreciates the irony that no matter how much money you have, you never feel rich. He knows this only too well. Rachel has been on at him for some time to get their house done up like the one next door; then there are the kids' university and school fees as well as those for his various private members' clubs; likewise, the restaurants, the cars, the holidays… The list of bills and expenses seems never-ending to Tony. These concerns cross his mind like restless black clouds as he strides through the airport, his moves automatic. Tony wants to get out of the terminal building as soon as possible. Fortunately, his flight is early and Heathrow has yet to fill with the mass of overnight arrivals. He clears passport control quickly and, moments later, Tony is on the train, speeding into town. Almost there, he thinks, his time in America already seeming an age ago.

In his youth, it had felt so different. Each trip had been exciting, and New York more than anywhere else. Then, its bright lights and its brashness were the allure, a visit being testament to having hit the big time. He had loved the feeling of being able to walk into places like the Pierre or the Plaza and state confidently that a room had been reserved for him, even though someone else would always have made the bookings. Now, it is just another city for Tony, a destination to pass through and do business in before moving on to the next location, a constant repetition of an all-too-predictable routine. Visits to anodyne office buildings are interspersed with waits in almost-identical airport lounges; sightseeing never part of the agenda.

Tony heaves a deep sigh. He is beginning to feel more depressed. His mood sours further as he devotes increased attention now to the information that is streaming across the screen of his phone. The financial markets have yet to open in London and elsewhere in Europe, but the indications are that his fund will lose more money when they do. None of the bets he has made on the market seems to be working; everything is going against him. His incoming emails inform him that one of his largest clients is requesting an urgent meeting. There is another from the regulatory authority notifying him that a representative will be visiting the office next week. It is just a routine check, Tony reads. Nonetheless, it worries him. A reminder then pops up, highlighting a meeting with a colleague later this morning. It is someone who has been threatening to resign for some time. Tony fears the worst. Everywhere he looks, there seem to be problems and difficulties, things he needs to sort out, be responsible for and arrange.

It never used to be this complicated, Tony thinks. He calculates that almost thirty years have now passed since he first worked in finance, a long graduation through a series of roles and firms that had culminated in him starting his own fund management business – TL Capital – two years ago; quite a journey. His initial opening had been obtained through an acquaintance of the family. Tony had been delighted to be given the opportunity to work as a junior stockbroker, although the sight of endless rows of desks populated by men shouting down telephones had initially daunted him. He had felt conspicuously out of place in his Marks & Spencer suit. But it was a rapid learning process. Everything had felt possible. There were no rules, no regimented processes. Most people, it seemed, made it up as they went along: "I've got a great tip for you. Trust me. It's a no-brainer. This one's a ten-bagger. You can't lose out. Everyone I know is getting into it!"

All you had to do, he quickly realised, was get on the phone and persuade strangers to buy and sell things that neither you nor they fully understood. Even if your recommendations to trade in certain shares were wrong – which was often the case – there would always be another day, another person who could be convinced easily enough to part with their money. Soon, he was getting his suits made in Savile Row, monogrammed shirts too. Tony realises now that he was part of a unique generation, one which had helped itself to the opportunities that were available. Everyone – both those working in finance and their clients – had been consumed by a shared dream of getting rich. There was, undoubtedly, a certain addiction attached to making money. Excess knew few limits at the time. An overbearing sense of self-confidence dominated. Time had moved on, however; things had changed. Everyone had been forced to grow up.

At the current moment, Tony wishes that he could return to this earlier, halcyon period. It was an age of innocence when he certainly had greater fun and fewer responsibilities. There were long lunches and generously forgiving expense accounts. A blind eye was generally turned to indiscretions. Stretching on the train's seat, Tony can feel the tension that has been building in his shoulders. The only lunch he'll get today will be stuffed down hurriedly at his desk – if he's lucky. He stretches again, then takes off his glasses, pinches his nose to relieve the stress, rubs his eyes and reluctantly begins to make a list of what he needs to do as soon as he gets into the office. Scrolling between his emails, taking notes as he goes along, Tony notices an unopened message from his father, which had initially escaped his attention. He had bought the computer as a gift for his Dad last year, but was not aware that he actively used it. Tony reads the mail: "Son, how are you? Jet-setting again, probably. I rang your home last night, but there was no answer. Stay well. Lots of love."

It is the brevity that affects Tony most. It forcefully reminds him of his dereliction of duty and so compounds his guilty conscience. Tony is aware that he has not seen his father for some time. It must be at least three months, he thinks. While his Dad remained in good health for now, he was not getting any younger. Every time Tony did see him, he seemed slightly more shrunken and cantankerous. Tony had promised that he would visit more regularly, especially after his mother had died a couple of years back. After all, his father had helped bring him up and still served as a role model, a solid, upstanding person with a strong sense of morals. Yet the commitments of work, holidays or more important social events always somehow got in the way. Tony realises these are poor excuses, flimsy and insubstantial, especially since his father lives so near to him. Tony recollects that he had always been taught the importance of his roots by his parents. Even though he has come far and lives a life that his father finds hard to imagine, Tony's past and his family's background are inescapably part of him. They matter to him and help define him.

His feelings for London are fuelled partly by the knowledge that this was the city that the Lecrowitz family had made their home, escaping from the pogroms of Eastern Europe at the turn of the last century. It was a place that had welcomed them and many other Jews, where they could continue their traditions relatively undisturbed. From Whitechapel, where his great-grandparents had first settled and established themselves as tailors, the family had moved westwards and upwards in the world, his father running an antiques business at Alfies on Church Street before retirement. When he was born, Tony's grandparents had still lived in the East End. He can recall his trips there as a boy, particularly the visits to the Bagel Bake or to Bloom's. The tastes of smoked salmon and salt beef are still fresh in his mouth as if it were only this morning that he had eaten there. They are fundamental parts of his childhood. So too are the warrens of Alfies Antiques where he would wander, often losing himself among the mix of collectors, bargain hunters, tourists, opportunists and locals. There he would see the remnants of other people's lives, their forgotten histories, different yet intermingled. Furthermore, Tony would observe how business was done. He witnessed the art of the dealers at work, their negotiation skills, and the subtlety in how they brought a transaction to a close. Their approach was a vivid contrast to the brusque shouts of the fruit and vegetable market traders stationed outside the antiques market. He had absorbed it all; the experiences serving him well once he had begun his career.

"Ladies and gentlemen, we will shortly be arriving at Paddington. Please don't forget to take your belongings with you when you alight." The sudden announcement from the train driver shakes Tony into the present once again. Familiar sights greet him. The Westway appears to his left, beginning now to fill with morning traffic. Underground trains trundle past. Tony stands, putting his phone into his pocket and reaching for his bag. Amidst all his other thoughts, he realises, for the first time, and with a wave of disappointment more than irritation, that there has been no message from his wife. He worries, as he does with increasing regularity, whether she may be having an affair. He has seen men ogling her, even flirting with her, and regretfully knows she likes the attention. But who wouldn't, thinks Tony, given Rachel's figure – the product of regular gym sessions with her different specialist personal trainers – combined with her taste for expensive clothes and regular trips for facials and manicures. He had offered to fly her out to New York last weekend, thinking Rachel would like the opportunity to shop in some different places and eat at a couple of new on-trend locations, but she had made several somewhat half-hearted yet mostly plausible excuses. Tony hardly knows where she is most of the time. He hopes that the surprise holiday he has booked for them to go to Venice at the end of the month will be a success. It is partly to make up for the almost three weeks he has just spent in America, a longer business trip than usual. At least, thinks Tony, she'll be there to welcome him when he gets home. Perhaps he should buy her some flowers at the station before getting his taxi.

Minutes later, sitting with a bunch of roses in the back of the cab, fast approaching his house on Blomfield Road, Tony feels his anticipation building. He sees the canal with its brightly coloured barges and then the white stucco-fronted houses sitting resplendently behind it. He is home. As the taxi putters along and finally draws to a halt outside his house, Tony's mood falls once again. Now it is not thoughts of work, his father or Rachel that deflate him, but simply the mess that his eyes are forced to confront. It appears to be everywhere, encroaching upon him and his property. His driveway is almost blocked by that grubby white van with the Strattons logo written across its side. A couple of men are unloading bricks from it and these are being stacked in piles on the pavement, while another workman is carrying them elsewhere. Nearby, a cement mixer is balanced precariously close to the kerb, churning out what looks like brown sludge. The work on the property next door, he has been told, might go on for another year. He fears it may take longer, since little evident progress seems to have been made during his time away. Worse, he has heard his neighbours on the other side talk of upgrading their property.

Tony does, however, feel a certain sympathy for the workers that seem to swarm over the site. He recognises that many of them are outsiders – like his own family several generations ago – not that *they* would ever think of someone like Tony as anything other than a Londoner. He admires their enterprise. Here are people, he thinks, willing to travel in order to make money, following the rational laws of business, their supply meeting the evident demand. Nonetheless, Tony does sense that the area where he lives is changing. Externally, its period houses do now look even grander, modified by the growing number of extensions and conversions, but internally, something more unquantifiable had been lost. *He* had moved here since the location was near both to where his parents lived and to the local synagogue. Even if neither he nor they were particularly religious, it still felt good knowing that their chosen place of worship was close by. His decision had pleased his parents too. Should they wish, they could gather easily for Friday night dinners. There was comfort in that knowledge. Things like this mattered to him and to his parents, feeling part of a community.

He is now at the front door. Tony turns the key in the lock and enters.

"Hi Rachel, I'm home," he shouts. "Did you miss me?"

There is no answer. He calls again. Nothing. Around him, he can hear no sound of movement in the house; the shower is not running, the coffee machine is not hissing. There is only the dull and insistent noise of drilling from next door. He is beginning to get a headache. Tony drops his bags on the floor. The flowers remain uselessly in his hand. He notices that the petals of several have already fallen to the ground. The post-it note stuck crudely to the mirror in the hallway catches his eye: "Gone to the gym. Brunch with Annabel after. Call you later, R," it says. Tony notes somewhat disconsolately that there is no mention of her having missed him, nor any reference that might signal the slightest hint of affection, not even the inclusion of a cursory 'x' after her initial. He feels almost like an after-thought in her life. He wants to unburden himself and tell her about his trip, his worries, and also the message he received from his father.

His phone suddenly begins to buzz in his pocket. Maybe it's Rachel, Tony hopes. Pulling it out, however, yet another wave of disappointment greets him. It is his colleague, the one whom he is due to be meeting later today. Tony can already picture the scene, envisage the man's complaints, his rehearsed resignation speech and his baleful request for a salary increase. Sod it, thinks Tony. He decides not to answer the phone; he can pretend his flight was delayed. Yes, that's a decent enough excuse, reasons Tony; no one in the office probably knows exactly when his plane is due to be landing. The longer he can avoid looking at how much money he is losing, and the further he can defer his meetings, the better. A seed of an idea begins to grow in his mind; at first slowly, then more rapidly. He *will* go for a swim; after all, that's what he had been planning to do earlier.

A renewed sense of energy comes to Tony. He is going to seize the day. Or at least the morning. Tony starts to realise the beauty of his plan – if he is in the water, he is uncontactable. From the hall, he takes the stairs two at a time, looks in one cupboard for his swimming trunks and another for a towel. There is no point in unpacking. That can wait until later. Tony decides not to bother showering; he can do it at the pool. He does have the foresight to grab a new set of clothes, noticing how rumpled his blue checked shirt and chinos look after a night sleeping in them. In the bedroom mirror, Tony briefly catches sight of himself. Thick black stubble covers much of his face. He has not shaved since the previous morning in New York.

"You look just like a little rabbi!" The memory of how his parents would lovingly mock his swarthy looks when he was younger rises to his mind unbidden. Then it hits him; he has an improved plan. He'll take the whole day off work and simply say to his colleagues that he was delayed in the States. That way, not only will he be able to have his swim, but even better, he will surprise his dad by visiting him after. Perhaps he can pick up some smoked salmon bagels somewhere on the way.

Walking out of his house Tony is excited by the childish simplicity of his actions. The charm of his design grows on him; he is playing truant for the day, doing something spontaneous and different, having an adventure. He decides to turn his phone off. It will serve Rachel right, Tony thinks, if she now can't contact him; the boot will be on the other foot, and she can wonder where he is for a change. And, as far as his colleagues are concerned, it is the small hours of the morning in New York. He will call them around noon and pretend he has only just woken up. On a whim, he decides he will head to the leisure centre close to where his dad lives.

Of course, he could swim at either the RAC or the Lansdowne Club. He has memberships at both, but it is neither the establishment privilege of the former nor the discrete Mayfair seclusion of the latter for which Tony is looking today. He is bored with them and with many of the people who frequent these places. He has no desire – particularly not this morning – to partake in the predictable conversations about the latest restaurant and gallery openings, trips to yacht parties in St Tropez and fashion shows in Milan. There was a time when he too would seek to ingratiate himself with such conversational gambits, gratuitously name-dropping and bragging about the latest places he had visited. Indeed, ever since he can remember, Tony has been an obsessive collector. Perhaps hoarding is in his nature he thinks; something to do with the fear of things being taken away, an unfortunate legacy from his family's past. When he was younger, football stickers had been his passion. He can recall the thrill of the chase, the trading with his school chums and the elation of being the first in the class to finish the album. Later, it had been music and the excitement of building a record collection, acquiring the latest releases before anyone else and finding valuable obscurities about which he could boast. Bluebird Records just off the Edgware Road had been a godsend. In his early days at work, the game to play had been bragging about the number of Michelin-starred restaurants visited. He can still list them now: Pétrus, La Tante Claire, Le Gavroche... As he had got older and settled into his house, Tony had begun to acquire collectible pieces of Murano glass, both from Alfies and when in Venice, scouring the internet and utilising his contacts. While they fill his home and please Rachel, these artefacts seem increasingly trivial to Tony. He finds himself thinking less and less about what he has and more of the things he has done, the people he has met.

It's been a little while since he last went to the leisure centre, but Tony pictures it perfectly. This was where he swam as a child, close both to his home and school. Tony visualises the austere 1930s exterior, the slightly faded look of the whole place. He can almost smell the damp and the chlorine of the place in his nostrils. Tony bets that nothing will have changed. Other memories come flooding back as he continues to progress down the Edgware Road towards the pool. This, he realises, is where his roots lie. There is Peter & Minos across the road on his left, the barber's where he would get his hair cut as a kid, except it was just called Peter's then. Peter is already attending to his first customer. Tony waves expectantly, but Peter does not see him. Next comes R. Agius on Tony's right, where he had bought a scooter with the money he received with his first bonus. It was a red Vespa, his joy and pride at the time, even if riding it had never ceased to worry his parents – "do take care Tony! And please wear that helmet." A few doors down, Tony passes Perfect Pizza, where he recalls having finished up on many a drunken night in the past. In the clear light of the morning, it looks less welcoming and more forlorn, empty of people, with the stacks of cheap metal furniture being the only presence in the place. Just a little farther lies the turning for Church Street. On one side is where Bluebird Records used to be; on the other, Tony can see the stalls of the market holders, mostly set up and ready for the day's business. He will have to come back this way later, passing Alfies in order to get to his Dad's house. He may pop in; there might even be some of his Dad's acquaintances there, still hawking their wares. It will be an even better surprise, thinks Tony, to arrive at his father's house not just with food but some interesting stories too.

A few steps more, and now, what is this? The wilting bunch of flowers tied to a lamppost is the first thing that catches Tony's attention. He remembers the roses he bought for Rachel earlier. They are probably lying on the bed, losing more petals. This image slips quickly from his mind as he is stopped, almost literally, in his tracks by the yellow police A-board that straddles the pavement. Its message is brutal, brief and unambiguous, the significance of its words reinforced by the black letters, all capitalised. The first two sentences read, "WE ARE APPEALING FOR WITNESSES. CAN YOU HELP US?" It is the next word that is, however, the most shocking, standing stark and solitary on a line of its own in a font larger than the rest of the text, to magnify its importance,

"MURDER"

Tony rapidly scans the rest of the information. He reads that, "ON FRIDAY 15 APRIL 2016 AT ABOUT 10.14PM A MALE WAS FATALLY STABBED ON THE EDGWARE ROAD." After this follows a number to call should any witnesses have seen anything. The idea of a murder happening in a location as familiar to him as this, a place he considers his home, shocks Tony to his core. It makes him pause.

Tony's initial thought is to wonder what he would have been doing at the time when the incident occurred. It does not take him long to work out that, of course, he would have been in America and probably stuck in a meeting. He then thinks of Rachel's whereabouts and whether she might have been nearby. He has no recollection at all of her mentioning the event on the few times they did actually speak while he was away. Moving on slowly from the police sign, Tony's mind drifts on to the broader topic of fate and the inexplicable nature of randomness. He has no idea how the person who was murdered came to be so, what might be his back story, his personal circumstances; also, what may have been his final thoughts and feelings as he lay there dying. Luck, or lack of it, plays a disproportionately large role in life, Tony muses. He thinks of how his family were fortuitous enough to escape from Poland more than a hundred years ago, but how thousands of other Jews would have perished there. He cannot forget this piece of history. Similarly, he feels that he will remain forever scarred by the fall of the Twin Towers. As they had crumbled to dust on a day with sky as blue as this one, Tony had watched open-mouthed and disbelieving, the commentary on the trading floor's television screens rendering the events more like those of a terrible movie than something that was happening in real time on the other side of the world. And, just yards from here, one of the train bombs in London had exploded back in 2005, shattering abruptly into many people's daily commute. That old sense of guilt, the feeling that it could have been *him*, sends an involuntary shiver down Tony's back. He then shivers again at another, related memory; of the eerie silence that pervaded the trading floor during the minute's commemoration held after these recent tragedies. The man who had died just here on the road would be remembered by fewer people, although their grieving would certainly be as deep.

All these thoughts and more continue to play deeply on Tony's mind as he approaches the pool. He pushes open the heavy doors – they are just as he recollects, only a bit stiffer – and enters. He's looking forward to his swim. In the water, he hopes he will be able to relax properly for perhaps the first time that day. After that, there is then the conversation with his Dad to anticipate. He will likely be a mine of information about the recent Edgware Road tragedy. With a sudden ache, Tony realises that he is longing to hear more of his Dad's knowledge, and stories too about his past, while there is still time. He also hopes that he will be able to share some of this knowledge with his own children. Even if they are more secular than he, and less conscious of history, Tony is keen to ensure that they have some awareness of where they come from, that they respect their roots. He is pocketing his change and is about to go through the turnstile when he turns to the girl behind the counter and asks if she knows anything about the incident that occurred up the road. She looks momentarily blank. Tony realises he is perhaps not explaining himself clearly enough. Of course, it happened almost three weeks ago. He has not had enough sleep and so much has already upset him since he landed this morning. Tony rephrases his question and is provided with the response,

"A boy got stabbed."

The news shocks Tony and he asks for more information, the age of the victim and the whether the girl at the counter knows the circumstances. He learns in a couple of sentences that boy was a teenager and that the reasons behind is death are uncertain, perhaps something to do with drugs. Tony thanks the girl and walks slowly on to the changing rooms. Yet he still can't get the image of the drooping flowers next to the police information board out of his mind. Now, he thinks of the life that was cut short, a teenager with so many years ahead of him. The boy, Tony realises, would have been about the same age as his children. One is at university, the other just finishing boarding school. They are already leading their own lives, developing their sense of independence. He *assumes* that they are sensible and can look after themselves, but then, of course, he does not know; did the parents of the murdered youth have any insight into what he was really up to?

Tony's next thought is that he cannot see a thing. He is in the pool's changing rooms and his glasses have immediately misted up as he is assailed by all the smells so familiar to him. He waits momentarily, pulls out a handkerchief and cleans his glasses. Vision restored, Tony surveys the scene. There are many people in various states of dress and undress, the early arrivals already finished, the next wave of pool goers just arriving. Some of the faces are familiar to him, others much less so.

"Morning all," Tony calls out in an attempt to sound more cheery than he feels.

A couple of people return his greeting or simply nod slightly in his direction.

"Ah," drawls the voice of Archie languidly. "Now, we haven't seen you here for quite some time."

Tony identifies him, remembers that he is a man who seems to have opinions – mostly inaccurate – on everything, likes the sound of his own voice and has that irritating habit of humming not only loudly, but also badly.

"Yup. Well I just got back from New York," responds Tony, hoping that this constitutes a satisfactory answer.

The next words emerge from his mouth almost unconsciously. Tony is not even aware that he is saying them. They are certainly not addressed to Archie specifically, more at the changing room in general.

"What's this I hear about a murder?" he asks. And then continues, clarifying as much to himself as to anyone else, "some silly kid getting stabbed over drugs just up the road."

There is a pause. Time rocks on its axis. A strange silence seems to fall on the changing room. Everyone appears to have stopped what they are doing, as if momentarily suspended and lifted out of their mundane activities and routines. Even the hairdryers are not running. In the distance, there is just the faint sound of splashing, though at this moment it sounds quite unreal to Tony's ears, almost as bizarre as the sight of the lone milk float he spotted earlier. He must be tired, he thinks.

It is, however, only the briefest of pauses, perhaps not even long enough for Tony to register that something might be wrong, and certainly not sufficient for Archie or anyone else to respond to his question. The next thing that happens is quite unexpected. In one swift movement Leon flings his towel on the floor with a heavy bump. There is no mistaking the noise it makes. Then, in one, two, three steps he is standing face to face with Tony. He is stark naked, fully exposed.

Tony is not sure whether it is drops of water from the shower or beads of sweat that glisten on the head of this man he barely recognises and has certainly never spoken to before. It is evident, however, that he is very angry. His fists are clenched, his muscles straining, his veins pulsing. It is clearly a struggle for him to control his breathing and remain calm. As he begins to speak, the effort to keep the emotion from his voice is evident for all to hear. The words come out with a forceful dignity. They change everything. Leon says, "that's my son you're talking about."

Interlude: Ishmina

Call me Ish – that's what my mates do. My full name is Ishmina Anabia Haddad. I'm 23 years old. Describe myself? Well, average height, but a little overweight, although since I've started using the gym and the swimming pool more regularly, the pounds have been falling off me. Soon, I'll hopefully be one dress size smaller, which is pretty exciting. My eyes are brown, similar in colour to the dates I adore eating. My hair is jet-black, long and thick. Not that you'll ever see it. Ah, I've got your attention now; you want to learn more, don't you? Well let me tell you, I am many things: young, confident and proud; a female, a Muslim and a Londoner.

However, when I sit here – at the leisure centre's reception desk – people look at me and they *judge*; they don't think. Instead, they form impressions based simply on appearance, making assumptions, without knowing anything about me. Wearing a hijab has nothing to do with religion or their opinion of feminism; it is not a form of emancipation or oppression. It is my right to dress how I want. And not be judged for it. I am an equal to men and wear what I feel like. There is so much they don't know. How, for example, my grandparents and their families were caught up in civil war, ripped from their homes in Beirut, and became part of an exodus in the 1970s from a once-great country. How they were forced to start new lives in London, learn a new language and integrate into a community that did not immediately welcome them. How I have come to understand that suffering, bigotry and prejudice are not new, but skeins that run unrelentingly through history. How my faith helps me overcome these and other everyday problems. How praying makes me stop, think and take stock of life in a world that is running way ahead of me most of the time. How I am doing a PhD on George Eliot (yes, a dead woman from the nineteenth century, but a heroine of mine: self-taught and fiercely independent) and only working here at the leisure centre three mornings a week to earn some extra money during my studies. How I am a young woman much like any other (I bleed once a month), with most of the same wants, needs and desires. I don't drink alcohol, but I still party with my friends, sit in coffee shops (the Middle East had a coffee culture long before the West), eat junk food, shop in Primark, have a Facebook account, post pictures on Instagram, watch videos on YouTube. How I can enjoy these simple pleasures, which a generation ago – and in a different country – would never have been possible.

I liken my role at the leisure centre to that of an onlooker, observing rather than participating in the lives of others. And a privileged onlooker too, for I see but am not always seen. Additionally, I know far more about the customers who pass through the turnstiles than they will ever do about me. I have not only the leisure centre's database with all their details in front of me – a quantum of information available at my fingertips in a couple of clicks which would have been unfathomable to George Eliot (perhaps more so even than the right for women to vote) – but my own eyes and ears too.

To me, this leisure centre and its pool are a perfect microcosm of London life, as diverse as anywhere in this amazing city: all ages, colours, professions and backgrounds, a vast swathe of intermingling cultures. It also has its patterns, its changing rhythms. They shift and stretch like a piece of fabric, as they have done throughout time. While I sit here, one group replaces another, yet something remains. I contemplate the pool behind me and wonder about all those who have swum here. What were their ambitions, hopes and fears; what secrets did they carry?

This morning I have been thinking about ghosts. As I walked to the leisure centre, I mused – as I often do – on whether I was retracing George Eliot's footsteps. Her diaries record her visiting regularly the post office and the grocers on Church Street. I wonder what she would have been thinking as she went about her errands; was it the mundane – what should she have for dinner; beef or mutton, with carrots or turnips – or the sublime, an idea for a new poem or story perhaps? George Eliot's is not the only ghost I contemplate as I walk the streets locally. There are many others here too; I have absorbed part of their histories, and now feel their presences regularly. I imagine Ben Jonson drinking at The Wheatsheaf, a long-forgotten pub that stood where there is now a bank on the corner of Church Street. He has a jug of dark frothing ale in one hand and maybe a quill in the other, brooding over the next lines of his play. I visualise William Shakespeare, acting as a strolling player – perhaps a mischief-ridden Falstaff – in the Red Lion, another now-absent pub, replaced by the harsh concrete of the Marylebone flyover. Then there is the tale of William Hogarth: he got married in the church just by the local college, where my youngest brother is currently studying. It was a scandal, a secret marriage, to the daughter of the man who taught him to paint. I picture the young Hogarth pacing the nearby streets, his fate in his hands, wondering whether he was making the right decision, and what impact it might have on his subsequent career.

There are also the blue plaques I pass regularly on the nearby roads, reminders of two illustrious women who made this area their home, paving the way for so many others, including myself. Just minutes from the pool lived Mary Seacole, a heroine of the Crimean War, who fought racial as well as sexual prejudice throughout her career. Meanwhile, one block further south was the house of Elizabeth Garrett Anderson, a woman who eventually became accepted in a male-dominated world, being the first in this country to qualify as a surgeon. I visualise them, going about their daily business (might they have known each other?), and try to imagine how it might have felt to overcome the challenges they did. Even if their legacies live on, the answers to my speculations will never be known; no search engine can capture all the minute details of such uniquely personal histories. So much remains unknown.

Jumping forward through time, I continue to wonder whether any of the Beatles ever swam here, when John Lennon lived around the corner. It would have been in 1968 – that's what the blue plaque says – at the height of the group's fame, the year they released *The White Album*. *Sergeant Pepper* had come out previously and *Abbey Road* followed soon after. They're all on my Spotify stream, the songs' lyrics in my head, along with the image of John, Paul and George larking about in the water (Ringo couldn't swim; this I know). Perhaps it was even here, at this pool, that they got the idea for *Yellow Submarine*. And what about Mandy Rice-Davies, one of the girls at the centre of the Profumo affair? From where she lived on Bryanston Mews, she would almost have been able to see the leisure centre. Did she come here to stay in shape, or perhaps later – after the headlines broke – to seek a place of refuge, an escape from the media circus that surrounded the scandal? I picture her swimming neat strokes in splendid isolation, alone but unrepentant.

Then there was the report of a drowning that occurred at the pool some years ago. I can't remember where I first about heard it – and there is so little information available online – but it has continued to play on my mind. The stark and disturbing image, of dead people – that's right, there was more than one – floating in the pool haunts me. I just can't get it out of my head. The story goes like this: back in the summer of 1995, a mother and her two young children were found fully-clothed and drowned in the pool, first thing in the morning. There were no signs of a break-in or struggle. The only conclusion I can draw is that they must have hidden in the changing rooms until the pool had shut the previous day. Perhaps it originally seemed just a fun game that the mother persuaded the children to play. Later, I imagine, they ventured alone and unsupervised into the deep blue waters, where the mother proceeded to drown first her children and then herself. But who can know for certain?

While I cannot see into the changing rooms, the bank of video cameras at my desk provides me with multiple perspectives of the leisure centre; I think of them as additional sets of eyes. In one I have a perfect (or almost perfect, since the screen is currently flickering) view of the pool, who is entering and leaving. No such technology existed at the centre back then. That family's terrible secrets – what could have brought a mother to murder her children in such a macabre and premeditated way – have sunk to the pool's bottom, probably never to be retrieved.

The tableau of the drowned family in the pool is there, unfortunately floating before me. And now I realise why. It was earlier this morning that one of the people who came to use the pool was asking me about another murder. According to my database, he is Tony Lecrowitz (an interesting surname; like me, he must have his roots elsewhere, another in the long line of those now sucked up and absorbed into this city), he's 48 years old and hasn't set foot in the leisure centre since last summer. I was originally confused when he asked whether I knew anything about the incident that had occurred up the road, since I hadn't noticed anything untoward on my journey into work that morning. There hadn't been anything interesting on my Twitter feed and certainly no anxious texts from family or friends checking whether I was OK. Clearly nothing dramatic had happened in the time I'd been sitting here. He must have noticed my confused expression, since he told me that he had seen a yellow police board halfway up the Edgware Road asking whether anyone had information about a recent murder.

I knew then what he was talking about, for it had been massive news at the time, though the event itself took place almost three weeks ago. Everyone was talking about it, so how could Tony Lecrowitz only just have heard? A young boy, about the age of my brother Salman, got stabbed just up the road. Things like that don't normally happen around here. It's a pretty peaceful area for central London. I think of the Edgware Road as a place of beauty, a street flanked by restaurants and cafes, their calligraphy scrolling from one country to the next, music pouring from the doors; not somewhere associated either with violence or drugs.

We discussed the murder quite a bit at home, given the way in which it had intersected with our own lives. Salman was pretty shaken up by it, as were most of his friends. While he didn't know the kid who got murdered – Samuel-something, I think he was called – they'd both been at the same college. My other brother, Abdul, was touched by the event too. He was back for the holidays from Oxford and was working, as he does most vacations, in the pizza place up the road; the one he always frequented as a teenager, and still hasn't quite grown out of. He wasn't there the night the murder happened, but it didn't stop the police from coming round a few days later and interviewing him, probing Abdul about whether he'd ever encountered the group of boys before, for it was apparently in Perfect Pizza that they had gathered before the fatal incident occurred. There was nothing he could tell the police – he had never seen any of them before. However, it was what Salman said that stuck with me. He was of the view that the boy's death had created a hole, or maybe more a vacuum, a space which could never be filled again. He felt that something had ineluctably changed at the college. I sort of know what he means. There is one more ghost now haunting the area.

Part Two: At the Deep

"That's my son you're talking about."

The words are uttered by Leon instinctively, automatically. They are not rehearsed, for how could they be? The thought of Samuel, his gaping and inescapable absence, the fact that he will never return, has not left Leon since his death. It is his affliction, one that he has carried unceasingly for almost three weeks. More than this though, the depth of his pain and anguish has remained secret, locked deeply inside; it is not something he has been able to unfold fully, not to his wife, and certainly not to friends or colleagues. Now, however, confronted by a stranger – and one who has had the gall to refer to his beloved son as a "silly kid" – Leon feels all his anger and more, his repressed emotions, on the point of being unleashed. They have been bottled up for too long.

An uneasy silence has fallen upon the changing room. It is a tableau of suspended animation. Everyone appears to have stopped midway through whatever action they were involved in. They are staring, fixated, unsure of what to do or what may happen next; bit-part actors in a play in which they did not choose either willingly or knowingly to participate. Leon, however, is about to erupt. Fist clenched and fury surging, he pauses, fleetingly, and observes properly for the first time, the man whom he is facing. He sees money in the expensive though wrinkled shirt, the smart trousers, the brown tasselled shoes and the designer glasses. By contrast, Leon realises for only the briefest of moments the absurdity of his own appearance – utter nakedness – his towel lying uselessly on the floor elsewhere.

Here Leon stands, undeniably exposed, both physically and emotionally, everything laid bare for all to see. Looking at Tony, Leon sees his greying hair, the lines on his face and the bags under his eyes. A fat golden wedding band glints on his finger. The man, Leon realises, must probably be about the same age as him. Perhaps he too has kids; if so, they might be similar in age to Samuel. How might this man feel – one who by the looks of it may never have known true hardship or adversity – were the very foundations of his life to be pulled from under him, his comfortable assumptions challenged, his child gone forever?

Leon does not get the chance to find out. The temporary suspense, where time seems to hang and float, as if in a void, is shattered by the sound of the changing room door opening. All heads, turn instinctively towards it. The movement of the door helps in some small but tangible way to diffuse the mounting tension between Leon and Tony. Both remain facing each other, Tony dazed, disoriented and lost for words; Leon fuming, his breathing heavy and his emotions awry. Neither has yet had a moment to consider what they may do next. Both are out of their depth.

In walks a young man. He is tall and callow, with limbs long, loose and awkward, as if he is not sure where to place them. He has floppy black hair and a face pock-marked with pimples, some a violent hue of red. His uniform marks him out as a member of the leisure centre's staff and his badge identifies him as Ignacio. He reluctantly drags a bucket and mop behind him. Ignacio is new to the job and already he dislikes it thoroughly; the cleaning of floors and toilets, the emptying of dustbins and refilling of dispensers. He relieves his boredom by daydreaming, planning when he can escape from this work and return home to Spain.

The sight of two men – one dressed, the other totally naked – standing inches apart in seeming confrontation is a novel one for Ignacio. Nothing so far in his brief time at the leisure centre has prepared him for this. It is not at all clear what he should do. Should he try to break them apart, or might this make things worse? Should he call his line manager and ask for help? Should he try and talk reason to them, even if his English is almost certainly not up to it? Should he just walk away, find somewhere else to mop, and come back to the changing room later? All these thoughts and more flash briefly across Ignacio's mind. He takes a couple of tentative paces into the room, lugging his bucket and mop behind him, hoping that these items help validate his presence, while additionally acting as some form of defence. No one has yet said a word. The sound of the changing room door shutting behind Ignacio echoes loudly. It seems to snap him, and everyone else, back into reality. Ignacio knows he has to do something…

… and so, he takes the easy option. "I'm sorry. I interrupt. I go now," he says, and shifts, ready to depart. He can return later, hoping that the whole incident will have passed and been forgotten; it is not his responsibility to sort out whatever these two men may be involved in. However, in altering direction, his plan made and his exit now decidedly rushed, the cleaner's bucket swings in an unfortunate arc. He has still not got the hang of moving the thing around; its four wheels seem to travel in conflicting orbits, refusing obstinately to coordinate.

The dampness of the changing room floor makes manoeuvring it even harder.

There is the sound of something falling. It is markedly different in cadence to the thud of Leon's towel, an action that now seems long distant, given how time has flexed. The noise that everyone hears – Ignacio too, paused in his tracks, despite his evident desire to be somewhere, anywhere, else – is that of an abrupt bang followed by a noise perhaps most similar to leaves being shaken from a tree during a storm, the flutter of many small things falling to the ground simultaneously.

The cleaner's bucket has inadvertently knocked over Archie's briefcase. In his haste to leave the house this morning, or perhaps absent-mindedly on the train into London, Archie must have left it unlocked, for now its papers are fanning across the floor, forming a bed of white on the checked tiles. Some are already turning soggy.

Archie is as unprepared for this outcome as anyone else. Barely a minute ago, he had been sitting there after his swim, towel pleasingly tied like a toga around his waist (imagining himself as a dignitary in Ancient Rome had tickled him), one leg crossed over the other, massaging expensive lotion onto his feet. He had originally loathed the lotion – another gift from Georgina – but has now become rather accustomed to its scent of lemon and bergamot. Both his hands and his feet are sticky, and he is therefore unable immediately to respond to the mess of his overturned briefcase, or to process the full implications of this event.

Ignacio is quickest to react. Flushed with embarrassment and shame, fearful that the incident may cost him his job, he simply wants to get as far away from the scene as possible. There is nothing he feels he can say that might make up for his error or remedy his ineptitude, so unfolding his long limbs, he bends down, and rapidly starts trying to scoop all the paper into a neat pile.

Both Leon and Tony are too bemused by this abrupt turn of events to respond. It seems so remote, too accidental to be related to their confrontation. They stand uninvolved, temporarily frozen once again. Ignacio is working as fast as he is able. Almost there, he thinks, just a couple more pieces – uno, dos, tres – and that's it. He has the bundle. The pages are mostly the right way up, he thinks, and only a couple appear to have been damaged by water, hopefully not that badly. In his confusion, however, the cleaner turns around and hands the pile not to Archie, but to Tony.

Tony's day feels increasingly strange to him. New York, even the plane, train and taxi back to his house, and then the journey to the pool, seem like worlds away, distant and unattainable. He feels tired, but more than that, immensely overwhelmed. The sight of the yellow and blue police board, the lone bunch of sagging flowers tied to the lamppost, is indelibly etched in his mind. Thoughts of what he wants to say to his father as well as his children next time he sees them continue to swirl through his head. Then there is the much more pressing consideration of how he should respond to the unknown and potentially violent man still facing him, whose son seems to be at the centre of this tragedy. Nothing makes sense to Tony, and now a pile of papers, which are certainly not his, has been thrust unwittingly into his hands. The action is too sudden and inexplicable for anyone else yet to have moved. Tony takes off his glasses, pinches his nose. He has no idea whose papers they are. Everything seems to have lost its bearings today. He squints and focuses. He murmurs, almost without realising and more to confirm what he sees rather than for the benefit of anyone else, the words "Crispin, Keagan and Smith."

There is a brief and uncanny pause. Time hangs suspended again. Then it shifts from one side to another and tips. Archie leaps abruptly from where he has been sitting. His neatly tied towel falls from his waist as he does so, revealing everything. Before any words issue from his mouth, he stretches, seeking desperately to reclaim his property, the papers that are *his*. They remain – for now – in Tony's hands.

The reaction of Leon is more notable and startling. Barely a minute ago, all his rage as well as his frustration and impotence to change what has happened to Samuel were channelled at Tony. Now, suddenly, his attention is focused intensely on Archie. For Leon, Tony had constituted a simple and almost unintentional outlet for his emotions. Archie, in Leon's mind, is a much more legitimate target. The two naked men now face each other, one radiating anger almost to the point of bursting, the other fear, confusion and also the dawning of an unfortunate realisation. Words again come to Leon automatically as he stabs his finger menacingly close to Archie's pale face. They are brutal and forceful, his conclusion immediately made from the evidence currently lying in Tony's hands: "You! You're one of those fancy lawyer types. Your firm is representing the bastard who murdered my kid. What do you know about tragedy? What do you know about the loss of a son?"

Leon's finger is inches from Archie's face. He can feel Leon's wrath pulsing alarmingly close to him. Archie's chest feels tight and his heart is racing; he hears its insistent beating echoing loudly. He worries whether he may be about to have a seizure. Archie loathes any form of physical violence and knows he would be useless in a fight, particularly against a man such as Leon. Words are his chosen form of defence, they always have been. Thoroughly out of his comfort zone, Archie has no other option but to think rapidly now what to say, before something much worse happens.

The truth of Leon's accusation rings in his ears. Even if said in rage, it has unwitting accuracy. That Archie *is* the man representing the accused perpetrator of Samuel's death must show on his face, in his trembling and fearfulness, as he stands facing the father of the victim. But, it is Leon's second assertion – what might he, Archie, know of tragedy – that hits him like a current of electricity, severe and vivid. Archie's next reaction is surprising, not just to him but equally to Leon, Tony and Ignacio (the cleaner is still uselessly present, frozen like a statue). It is impossible for anyone in the changing room not to observe Archie's decline. In the opposite corner, Mariusz stands, as transfixed as Ignacio. He is petrified and hopes desperately that no one will notice how he has turned even paler than Archie. Other forces are taking direction in his life.

They all watch as his shoulders droop suddenly and then Archie crumples, sinking to the floor as if struck by some terrible, unspeakable, condition. Archie buries his head in his hands and begins to cry. It is an appalling noise, a cross between gulping, moaning and whimpering. He sounds like he is struggling to breathe. Between heaving convulsions, some words emerge from Archie's mouth. They are mumbled, yet still loud enough for everyone to hear, dropping like cold stones into the changing room: "My son died too. Seventeen years ago." Memories do not fade; incidents resurrect them.

In a rush, Archie is jolted into the distant past as all the events of that time, the birth – and death – of his first child, come rushing back to him in a painful and violent flood. They had started trying to conceive after around a year of marriage and Georgina had got pregnant without difficulty. Archie's excitement, admittedly combined with a certain degree of trepidation, had mounted with each event preceding the birth: the missed periods, the positive pregnancy test with its twin blue lines, the visit to the doctor which confirmed the outcome, and then the scans. They were informed that it would be a boy. Next came deliberations over possible names. Eventually Herbert was settled upon; Georgina's enforced choice, in homage to her deceased father. Every subsequent stage of the pregnancy was approached with almost military precision and organisation, items meticulously checked off a lengthy list, from deciding which pram to purchase (although he played no role in this) to painting the nursery blue ("let's get a man in to do the job," Georgina had said). Georgina managed capably throughout, even at the birth. Despite Herbert arriving three weeks earlier than anticipated, her birthing plan had been long written, her going-away bag already packed, and she had known what to do as soon as her waters broke. The labour was both swift and unproblematic. Within hours of arriving at the hospital, Georgina and Archie were allowed to hold their small child for the first time.

Prior to Herbie (as Archie took immediately to calling him), Archie had never thought of himself as a natural father. He had always been rather awkward around babies, and small children more generally. They constituted an unknown and often bothersome presence, lacking in routine and mostly prone to irrational behaviour which could not be quantified. He never quite knew what to say or do; irritated by the fact that he could not reason cogently with them. Yet, with Herbie, Archie was a man transformed. Sure, there were endless sleepless nights and dirty nappies, even if they did have a nanny (not negotiable as far as Georgina was concerned). However, the natural, elemental joy of seeing his son in the mornings before work, and in the evenings when returning, was like nothing he had ever known before. He awaited the weekends eagerly, counting down the time on a Friday before he could return home and dote adoringly on Herbie. Every gurgle, every gesture, would bring a smile to Archie's face. Archie could already envisage the wonderful future his son would have. In his mind's eye, he pictured Herbie in cricket whites, going up to his father's Alma Mater in Oxford and having the glitteringly successful career in law that had thus far eluded Archie.

Then came the fateful day. It was a Sunday, exactly sixteen weeks after the birth, and a moment he would never forget. The clarity with which Archie recalls the event is as if it had happened yesterday, the images cruelly imprinted on his brain, ineradicable. The nanny did not work at weekends, Georgina was heading out for a long-arranged lunch with a friend and so Archie had been left at home with Herbie, not that he minded, since it would mean time alone with his son. He had been fed before Georgina's departure, she had put him down for his nap and Archie was provided with strict instructions.

"I will be home by three Archibald, but *please* don't forget to wake Herbert (not Herbie; Georgina always frowned slightly at the abbreviation) and offer him his bottle. Surely you can manage that?"

"Yes, Georgie; trust me, I'll be able to cope."

When Georgina eventually left, having repeated her instructions to Archie again, he had sat contentedly at the kitchen table with a pot of Darjeeling, laboriously completing the newspaper's cryptic crossword. The minutes passed quickly, and he was soon mounting the stairs to raise Herbie.

The moment Archie entered the room, he knew that something was fundamentally wrong. Fear had rushed through him with such immediate force that he was trembling. Herbie looked strangely still. One arm was dangling from his cot. His flesh was deadly white except for a few purple blotches where the blood had settled. What had been warm and sentient barely two hours ago was now cold and stiff, a surreal monstrosity. Worse, everything that had been there previously, that Archie had considered forever his, was gone – in the blink of an eye. He had felt piercing and painful shock of a primeval sort, but more than that, hopelessness and utter despair. Somehow, drawing on instinctive reserves he had never previously known he possessed,

Archie had made it to the phone and called the emergency services prior to contacting Georgina. The arrival of not only the paramedics, but the police too, was swift. Soon the house had become an emergency zone. Police tape was already covering the premises as Herbie's tiny and shrunken body was carried away, even before Georgina had made it home.

The sense of absolute awfulness had never waned. Every time Archie brought it to mind, he could feel his own body tightening, constricting around him as if all its air were being squeezed out. That there was no rational explanation for what had happened only compounded matters. Georgina, of course, blamed Archie, since she felt he should have checked on the baby. Archie, similarly, had believed Georgina to be at fault, since she was the last person to have seen Herbie alive, when she had put him down for his sleep.

It was then, amidst unresolved arguments and unspoken resentments, that their emotional distance, the sense of his inadequacy in her eyes, first developed. Later, it widened, gradually yet inexorably. Among their circle of family and friends (or particularly Georgina's), it was not the done thing to discuss such matters.

"Keep a stiff upper lip Archie old boy," he had been told by Magnus a few days after the event.

"But…"

"No buts, Archie. Life has to go on. You've got your work to keep you going. And a good swim will be just the ticket to clear the mind."

"Magnus, you're missing the …"

"Come on, less of that Archie. Let me buy you another whisky."

Meanwhile, Georgina's emotions at the time had veered between the bitterly seething – at seeing "normal" (her word) babies all around them, being pushed by happy parents in their prams – and the fervently desperate. Her utmost priority, as she made abundantly clear to Archie, was to have another child as soon as possible; a Herbie replacement, a new object for her affections. Fortuitously, this wish was granted and Roger was born within a year; Jemima followed two more after that.

However, for Archie, it was all very different. A deep and unyielding sorrow had seeped into his bones and never dissipated. He dearly loved his other children, but they would *never* be a substitute for Herbie. His smile, which everyone had remarked could brighten a darkened room, had been replaced by darkness of an absolute and very different sort. The circumstances of his death were undoubtedly the most traumatic event that had ever occurred to Archie, wreaking irreparable devastation. He had *seen* the whole thing. It was he – and not anyone else – who had been confronted by the sight of his dead child, face flat on the mattress, cruelly squashed, as cold and solid as a block of ice. It was he who had to deal with the paramedics, the arrival of the police and their blue and white tape, treating his house as if it were a crime scene, Archie as if *he* were a criminal. Such had been the incoherence of Georgina's grief at the time, she remembered little of the day's events.

Like the faded and wrinkled photo he still keeps of Herbie in his wallet – hidden, yet always there – Archie has carried these terrible realities with him like a leaden weight. They have been his burden, which he has borne continuously; an indestructible sadness. His escapism, his swims,

147

his nocturnal forays, his interest in other people's lives – their tragedies diminishing his in some macabre way – have all been Archie's way of managing. Yet, he has never been able to explain this fully to Georgina, evidence of feeling being considered morally demeaning, a taint on practical manhood.

With the arrival of their other children, Georgina had thrown herself unreservedly into parenting and had seemingly forgotten about Herbie, or so it appeared to Archie, almost as if it were in some way distasteful even to contemplate the matter. However, images of their first son have never ceased to haunt Archie. Memories of him would come often unbidden and at the most unexpected moments. Sometimes it would simply be the sight of a tiny baby on the street, or the name Herbie called innocently to a stranger nearby. At other moments, it might be a certain shade of mottled purple, or the smell of Darjeeling tea. Time has not healed Archie; he has just become slightly more proficient at coping. The loss and grief are always there. Leon's words have unlocked these concealed and cruel emotions, forcefully and dreadfully. Like the breached defences of a dam, something has broken inside Archie.

The sight of a naked and quivering man dramatically keening on the floor is a horrific and dreadful one from which it is impossible to draw away. No one has intervened. A sense of embarrassment and fearfulness hangs uneasily in the air. Leon's hands drop to his sides, his fists unclench, and he breathes out heavily. Tony – still holding Archie's disintegrating papers – quietly clears his throat. Even with his poor grasp of English, Ignacio can appreciate the gravity of the situation. With it comes a decision, formed on the spot; he will hand in his notice immediately and return to Spain. This is not something *he* signed up to.

While Ignacio's thoughts are of escape, both Leon's and Tony's turn to their respective children. Archie's desperate and plaintive words reverberate in their ears. Leon once again pictures Samuel: as a baby, a toddler playing on the beaches of Trinidad, a boy in his Rangers jersey leaping for joy at a goal scored, and a teenager, fiercely independent, on the cusp of becoming an adult, yet still so young. All these memories will be cherished and treasured forever. Leon knows about the pain of loss, the gaping and irreplaceable vacuum that death brings; he has felt more than anyone, or so he believed. Yet he now thinks also of his twin daughters, currently with Joy in Nottingham. The image of their smiling faces, their non-stop chatter, the instinctive way in which one always knew what the other was thinking, strikes him with a sudden and guilty flash. He *knows* that he has neglected them. Samuel's absence, he realises, has crowded out all other emotional feelings. Archie's collapse, inches from Leon, is a reminder, a siren call, to return to his family. He can't replace Samuel – that is impossible – but he has his other children, and his wife. *They* are vital and precious to him too. Tony travels a similar arc. The pressures of work and how much money he has made or lost, the quantifiable metrics used for judging success and failure, are rendered trivial against thoughts of the uniqueness and importance of his children. He is hit with the forcefulness of this insight and feels an intense urgency to see them, to talk to them, both his son and his daughter, to hug them and reassure them that even if he has often been absent (they in boarding school and now one at university; he, away regularly for work) that he admires and adores them, loves them unceasingly. To lose one, he thinks, would be utterly unimaginable, beyond comprehension.

Archie's emotional disintegration renders this thought starkly unambiguous. Yet it similarly brings the realisation – independently to Leon and to Tony, for neither has spoken – of just how little they know, how quick they have been to judge; how they are but small parts of a huge, diverse and infinitely complex cosmos. You might see people such as Archie at the leisure centre, observe their superficialities and detest their mannerisms, but know nothing of their background and inner motivations. Their emotional state, whether they had argued or made love before coming to the pool, was of no conceivable relevance. In the shower or the changing room, their nudity would be visible, but their true thoughts and feelings hidden; the swimming pool constituting a solitary place, somewhere to be free, away from the pressures of daily life. Now everyone had been brought together, hitherto individual existences forced into abrupt and unwanted collision. Alone yet together, together yet alone; yes, that's it, thinks Tony.

The hideous and utterly unforeseen nature of the day's events makes their impact even worse. Tony realises that none of this would have happened had he chosen to visit a different pool rather than acting on a wilful impulse; had he taken a taxi to the leisure centre rather than walked; had he been less observant on his journey, or just arrived at a slightly different time. For the second time this morning he is reminded of the disproportionate role played by chance, the fickleness of luck, or lack of it. Leon arrives at a not dissimilar conclusion; only a few more lengths in the pool could have averted this outcome. Both now want to be anywhere other than where they stand – Leon naked, Tony in the clothes he has not changed out of since New York – in an increasingly claustrophobic changing room, floundering, out of their depth, and utterly unprepared to deal with the situation they face.

Neither Leon nor Tony has made eye contact with the other; to do so would be an admission of complicity or alliance, a notion alien to them both. Yet they remain united by the simple fact that their vision has not strayed from the pitiful sight of Archie. He has not said a further word and remains collapsed, shuddering, weak and defenceless on the pool's floor, his tears merging with its sticky dampness. He is oblivious to the presence of others, engulfed for now in his own deeply personal grief. His head almost touches his overturned briefcase, his bottle of lotion stands forlornly on the changing room bench; physical objects of importance moments ago, but useless and irrelevant now.

Leon responds first. Thoughts of violence are now far from his mind as he takes a step towards Archie and places a hand on his shoulder. It is a brief and simple gesture, natural, instinctive and intentionally consoling, not that Archie notices. Hand removed, Leon turns, keeping his head lowered and eyes focused on the ground. He has no desire to prolong this awkward and painful exchange any more than necessary. The sight of his towel, a vestige from what seems like a different era, reminds him of the need to get dressed and attempt to regain some semblance of normality.

Still clothed, Tony knows with definitive clarity that he will *not* go swimming; it would be too strange, incongruous even, after all that has happened in the few minutes he has been in the changing room. Whereas it was the cleansing solitude of the pool, its space and its silence, that he had craved first thing this morning, now all he desires is company. Tony looks towards the changing room door and the prospect it offers, an exit to a simpler world, one of buses travelling up and down the Edgware Road, share prices flashing red and green on computer screens and people living their lives unencumbered by the events he has just witnessed. He is about to leave when he realises Archie's papers remain in his hands. It feels as if they have been there for an eternity. Tony edges closer to Archie and places them on the bench beside him. He is on the point of departing when he bends and retrieves Archie's fallen towel from the floor and places it gently around his shoulders, as if Archie were a child, his child, in need of comfort. Archie seems unaware, just as he is of the sound of the changing room door banging shut. Tony has left, Ignacio too, in a rush, bucket and mop abandoned. Archie remains, similarly abandoned. In the distance, only the sound of the pool's waters echo, merging with Archie's anguish.

*****

The pool's waters echo in John's ears. They're awfully painful. He can't hear properly out of the left one. His eyes are red and stinging. His heart is racing and his chest feels tight as if there is something in it which needs to be expelled. John worries he might be about to vomit.

He is not used to physical exercise. What he'd like more than anything now is a sit-down with a cigarette and cup of sweet milky tea.

Although John now feels rather wobbly, he surprised himself by managing almost thirty minutes in the pool. As he had first stood on the water's edge in his baggy gym shorts he had felt nervousness akin to his first day at school, a fear of being discovered and exposed, as a fraud or, worse, a failure. John had never liked swimming. Just being by the pool, seeing the movement of the water and inhaling the smell of chlorine had been enough to bring a churning to his stomach followed by a distinct sense of nausea. With these sensations came a flood of unfortunate memories, such as the occasion he had first been made to swim without armbands.

"What's the matter John? It's easy. You're not a baby any more. Or are you?" one of his brothers had said.

The scorn and casual complacency of his siblings contrasted with his own abject fear of being alone and unaided in the water. Aged five, he had been convinced he would drown; he had felt he would burst into tears at any moment. Then came the moment of being thrown in at the deep end.

"Oi! You there with the ginger hair. Let go out of that child you're holding on to. You should know better." The brutal admonishment from the lifeguard still rang in John's mind now as he pictured how he had flailed desperately, almost dragging the child nearest to him under in the process.

"Baby! Loser! Accident!" followed from his brothers, accompanied by cruel laughter.

Meanwhile his Dad had remained standing in the spectators' area, scowling, shaking his head with undisguised disappointment.

Worse had followed in his school days. There was the ritual humiliation of being forced to dive into the water in front of his mocking peers. In races, John would finish last, his shame compounded by the knowledge that, next week, the process would likely be repeated. In the changing rooms, wet towels would be flicked at him, his shirt often drenched and his bag regularly hidden. "Whale, whale, you're so pale," became the incessant chant struck up by the other boys, an unfortunate but not entirely inaccurate nickname which stuck to him, like a barnacle.

He had thought about turning back and giving it all up. John had not been in a swimming pool since school and, prior to his unplanned decision this morning, had no intention of ever returning; surely to do so, of his own volition, would be a form of masochism. But, as he stood nervously by the side of the pool, John took in his surroundings. There was no teacher barking commands, no spectators, no one there whom he knew or who knew him; no one to judge, criticise or mock. And, sure, there was a fast lane were pounding effortlessly up and down, but also a slow one, not as narrow or crowded as the others. As he looked more carefully, John could see that the people here were not all engaged in some needlessly repetitious form of racing; rather, some were simply standing, others chatting. A few were using floats, and most looked like they were enjoying themselves.

That swimming might be a pleasurable experience had never previously occurred to John. Still sceptical, but committed now, eventually he summoned up the courage, climbed cautiously down the steps and took the plunge, flopping into the pool. John had willed his arms to move through the water while kicking his legs simultaneously. It was enforced survival, an automatic set of movements. He had willed himself on to the end, counting each stroke and praying fervently he would make it. He did, heaving a mighty sigh of relief, pausing to get his breath back and checking to see if anyone was staring at him, incredulous at his ineptitude. The other swimmers, however, were going about their business, barely registering John. Emboldened, he had turned around, rolled onto his back and kicked his way to the opposite end.

Soon, John had established a sort of rhythm, moving up the pool on his stomach, returning on his back. He found himself relaxing, feeling the waters lap over him, cleansing him. He began to forget about his school days, his family, his thankless job. Instead, he started thinking about happier things: the hills in Shropshire, the conversations he used to have with his Gran, the possibilities that London might offer him once he got more settled. Maybe he would come to the leisure centre more regularly, John had thought; maybe, he could make some friends, or go with Lucy – the girl he'd met handing out leaflets yesterday – for, surely, she would be impressed by someone who could swim.

Just as it was the thought of possibly seeing Lucy again that had driven John to the leisure centre that morning, so it is her image that summons him out of the pool. John pictures her blonde hair, her engaging smile and just how friendly she had been to him. If he encounters her, and John feels confident that he will, then he will tell her of his intention to make a new start and join the gym. She would like that. From there, he convinces himself, asking her on a date would be easy.

John showers rapidly, partly since he has forgotten to bring any shower gel but also given his desire to see Lucy. He returns to his locker. It is now just a matter of getting his clothes on and then he will see her in the lobby, he's sure. It *will* turn out to be a lucky day after all. John is in a rush now, pulling on his pants first, next his top. It's a pity that he was wearing it at work last night and that it's a bit grubby with pizza grease. As he struggles in haste, John gets his head stuck. It is submerged in the folds of his polo shirt when he hears the sound of something heavy hitting the ground nearby, like a wet slap. By the time his head has emerged, tentative like a tortoise's from its shell, John sees the angry man, whose dour look he had earlier avoided, confronting someone else.

John stares, transfixed and determined not to miss a moment. He feels it is his right, his just desserts, to be present, since he missed the stabbing incident that happened so close to his work a few weeks ago. If John understands correctly what is happening – and he is pretty sure that he does – then the father of the murdered kid is standing feet away from him in the changing room, stark naked and about to punch a stranger. Now, something exciting is finally happening to him; or, luckily, not *actually* to him, since he certainly wouldn't want to get in a fight with either of these men. But, he is getting to witness it all; he will have a story, an anecdote, something with which he can impress people. He will be able to tell his family, his colleague Abdul, and Lucy too, that he was there; he saw everything; not just the two men squaring up, but the incident with the cleaner, the next confrontation and then the collapse and tears of the man who had stared nosily at him earlier too.

Although it is his first time here, John cannot believe that such a chain of events is normal and might occur during a typical morning in the leisure centre. He wonders momentarily if he has been having some form of bizarre delusion, perhaps induced by the unusual amount of exercise he has undertaken. Yet, the emotion and the anguish he has just witnessed are unavoidable, as raw and as personal as the absence John feels when he thinks of his Gran. He misses her bitterly and wishes she were here now; she would have wise words to offer in this situation. Thoughts of her, her kindness and warmth, that she was there for him when others were not, bring a sprinkle of tears to John's eyes. He rubs them furiously, wanting no one else to see. The chlorine stings terribly, reddening them. John blinks and then two strange and unrelated things happen simultaneously.

Leon, having turned away from the pitiful sight of Archie, is striding towards John. He has not glanced at John's face, does not see the fear in his still-moist eyes. John is quaking, wondering what he may have done to provoke this man whom he does not know. Leon's focus is single-minded, his look unwavering. Now, it is not his discarded towel for which he is searching. His attention is centred on the logo he has spotted on John's shirt. There is a combination of outrage and confusion in his voice as he cries, "what the fuck?" At the very same moment, John feels a quivering hand on his shoulder and hears an elderly voice, slightly hoarse, yet full of disbelief and almost breaking with emotion, exclaim, "Alf! What are you doing here?"

Bert is convinced that it *is* Alf; he'd swear blind. He would recognise that ginger hair, pale freckled skin, slightly stooped and hunched look anywhere. It's occupying all his vision, obscuring the rest of the changing room. He's seen it hundreds of times in his life; at school, larking around in the park, on the beach when the four of them – Iris and Jean too – would go away to the seaside. But Alf had never been any good at swimming. He'd struggled in water, had always seemed fearful about drowning and had been the butt of many jokes, forever finishing last in races. When they'd gone on holidays together, Alf barely ventured into the sea. "I'll keep an eye on the ladies while they sun themselves;" or "ice creams on me, back in a bit," he might say. Meanwhile, Bert would swim confidently out, delighted to be in the waves yet disappointed that his mate had not joined him, could not share in his pleasure. Yes, Bert is sure, Alf hates swimming. So what could he possibly be doing here in the pool's changing room?

Confusion reigns in Bert's mind. Although it's still early, he feels like it has already been a long and difficult morning. He'd woken up with that recurring dream about being in the mountains with Iris, the one that always upsets him. On his walk to the pool a bit later, restless images – something to do with a murder and other thoughts too, relating to a man named Windrush Bob – had swirled uncomfortably in his mind, getting all mixed up. He'd been looking forward to his swim, since he felt going in the water would do him good and calm him; but by the time Bert had arrived at the leisure centre, he had already been feeling drained and unsteady. Then that strange and overly inquisitive man had leered at him in the changing room and ranted about stolen lockers. None of it made any sense. Bert didn't want to admit it, but he knew nonetheless that the fuzz in his brain was growing daily, eating away at his memories and, crucially, his confidence too. After changing, even the pool's waters had initially seemed threatening to him, swirling uncomfortably, as he stood by their edge. His aged body had reluctantly entered the water, but it was only after several lengths that Bert had felt the familiar ease of repetitive and intuitive movement beginning to have an effect, soothing his tangled emotions. Now, he didn't need to *think* about what he was doing. With the regular comforting motion, the tumult of the morning began gradually to diminish, retreating to a more distant spot, as Bert's thoughts turned to better times, those of a different era.

Alf had been in his memories, as he often was. Bert struggled to think of a time when he hadn't known him. They'd sat next to each other on their first day at school, struck up a friendship then and remained best mates ever since. Bert could recall it all. He brings to mind their time together at the local primary: the trips to the freezing boys' lavatories in the wooden shack next to the playground; wet play times in the coke store since there was nowhere else for them to go; gas lights in the classroom along with the meagre stove that burned in the corner; and, of course, the terrifying teachers. The boys had formed an automatic bond, united in the face of authority. After school had finished for the day, he and Alf had hung out too, mostly on the swings at the playground but then, as they had got older, all around the Church Street vicinity. Yes, they had ruled the roost there. It had obviously helped that Terry, Alf's Dad, had a stall on the market, but the community was small; they knew everyone. Alf had been a real character, a bit of a scallywag, a foil to Bert's more cautious self.

"Anyone watching us Bert?"

"No Alf."

"OK, here goes. One, two, three: right, I've loosened the tops of the vinegar bottles. Now all we have to do is sit back, watch and wait. It'll be a laugh."

"What if someone spotted us?"

"They didn't Bert. Just act normal and eat your chips. Don't look so worried."

"Here comes a punter now. Any moment…"

"Ha! You see that, Bert?! Half the bottle of vinegar over his chips. Now let's scarper!"

There had been many other similar japes, often played at the expense of unsuspecting strangers. Alf would also run dodgy errands for his Dad and his mates, taking their bets to the bookies lurking shadily in doorways, returning later when there were winnings to be collected. At least this served him well when he dropped out of school and started working in the local Ladbrokes once betting was finally made legal. Their friendship had endured into adulthood. Bert and Alf's wives had also been friends and the quartet they formed was as thick as thieves, going out to a dance hall or perhaps to see a show, sometimes just for an ice at the parlour on the Edgware Road or a glass of beer locally. Even when Alf and Jean's child had been born, they would still all knock about. They'd had a girl. Now what was her name; S-something? It would come back to him. She'd eventually grown up and moved away (the first of the family to go to college – hadn't her parents been proud?), and then it was just the four of them again, returning to the same old routine; less dancing now, but still fry-ups in the Metropolitan and pints in the Richmond. The pub had become their second home; they'd be there for birthdays, Christmases, events of any kind; even wakes…

Come to think of it, Bert realises, there'd been a wake recently. He'd gone to it, putting on his shabby tie and ancient suit for the occasion. Now, whose had it been? It couldn't be Ernie or Ned. He was *sure* they were both alive, since he'd seen them only the other day, shared a roast and natter with them at the cafe on Church Street, sitting at the same table they always occupied. It surely couldn't have been William or Ronald, since both of them died ages ago. No, it was none of them; rather, it was a woman; he's convinced. Bert can picture her, an image of her face forming before him. Light brown eyes, hair a similar colour before it turned grey, always a wonderful smile and a lot of laughter. Julie Andrews, that was it. No, hang on, wasn't she a film star? It can't have been her. Someone who looked like her. Of course, damn it, how could he have forgotten? It was Jean's wake he had attended at the

Richmond. But, if they had all gathered for Jean, then why was Alf not there?

The thought then crashes into Bert's mind with sudden and appalling abruptness: Alf died before Jean, ages before. He was one of the first of the gang to snuff it; it must have been a good ten years ago by now. It was a heart attack, wasn't it? That's right, but then again, Alf had always been a big drinker, had smoked like a chimney; liked a full English in the morning, pies at lunch and the odd saveloy from the stall on Church Street. His job was a sedentary one too, sitting behind the counter at the bookies, not standing out in the market and hefting things around come rain or shine like Bert did. But – and this is the more shocking realisation for Bert – if Alf is dead, then whose shoulder is his hand resting on?

Bert feels faint. With his free hand, he steadies himself against the wall of the changing room. Or at least he thinks it is a wall, as Bert wonders momentarily if he is perhaps back in the pool, since the tiles look as though they are moving, almost swimming, below his feet. Deep-seated fear rushes through him, uncertainty and utter confusion; it's all a terrible muddle. Bert is *convinced* he has seen Alf recently. It was definitely him, in his coat by the door just inside Bert's flat only the other day. However, by the time Bert had crossed the hallway, the image had disappeared, the empty shell of his own jacket hanging there alone, where it always had done.

If only Iris were here, Bert thinks desperately; she would be able to solve this puzzle. She was the sensible one, the person who could clear this mess up and dispel the terrible haze. That quack he'd seen had been useless. He'd never gone back for another appointment, couldn't see the point; he didn't want to take any new-fangled drugs or visit a so-called specialist who might make things worse for him, maybe even send him into a home. Although, hold on, wasn't there that thing the doctor had said? That's it, that there were those funny things he was told he might experience, images that were there one moment, clear as day, and then they were gone, in a puff, just like that. Now what were they called; bally-something-or-other; maybe pally-, or hally? Bert doesn't get a chance to finish his ponderings since the man he *thinks* is Alf, this moving, breathing, living person who is definitively *not* a hallucination, turns around and faces him.

John turns away from Leon. It is an instinctive reaction, like that of a fearful and trapped animal seeking to avoid a predator. He has no idea why the father of the murdered boy is staring so indignantly at him. John wonders what he can possibly have done to upset the man; how it is just his luck that he always ends up being the victim, the fall-guy, the sucker, the loser (the cruel laughter of the girls in that Shropshire pub echoes in his head). It is a depressingly familiar situation.

For the briefest of moments John's spirits lift. He thinks – no, hopes, desperately – that perhaps, just perhaps, the man's glare is not directed at him but at the person who has tapped him on the shoulder. Maybe he is involved in some way in all these strange events. Perhaps none of this is anything to do with John, but how can it be? For what John sees, now that he has shifted position, is a trembling, old and defenceless man. His body is withered and shrunken. Wrinkled skin sags from his arms. A few tufts of white hair are plastered to his head. Liver spots and protruding veins cover his hands.

However, it is his face which is the most appalling sight. It is not the bloodshot eyes, the broken veins on the nose or the missing teeth in the gaping jaw, but simply the expression. Bert's look reflects the realisation that it is clearly *not* Alf in front of him, but some stranger, an unfamiliar and potentially malign presence. It is a picture of turmoil, exhibiting fear; but more than that, weakness, panic and disorientation. John recognises all these emotions, for they mirror what he feels. Yet, there is something else; John is sure he's seen this old man before.

He's never been that good at remembering people, but there is undoubtedly something familiar about the quivering man opposite him. Maybe he's one of those strange, probably homeless people John has spotted shuffling aimlessly along the Edgware Road or lurking in the underpass clutching a bottle of spirits, sometimes accompanied by a shopping trolley containing their worldly possessions. Or perhaps John's seen him in the Green Man, slowly nursing a pint, or alternatively huddled over a small bag of chips in the place where he works.

The name the man called him, Alf, sits stubbornly in John's mind, nagging insistently at him. The penny drops. Alf! Why had he not thought of it before? Of course, that was the name of his Grandad. Obviously not Colin, his Dad's dad, a sour man whose only pleasure seemed to be to criticise others as he sat and opined from the brown armchair in the Telford bungalow which he never left, but his Mum's dad. John had liked him; his jokes, sly winks and that trick he had of making sweets appear out of nowhere. It was always a pleasure seeing him, though the visits were infrequent (sadly the same could not be said of the Telford trips), and John reckons he would have just started secondary school when his Grandad died. He doesn't remember it too well, but recalls it was a heart attack, massive and abrupt. There was never a chance to say goodbye.

John's thoughts lumber on; so, if Alf is my Grandad, then… this man must think I am Alf. The family likeness between them was unquestionable. Why, he'd only been looking through the photo albums he'd found in his Gran's flat the other night. They shared the same ginger complexion and large (what his brothers would unkindly call fat) build. Countless pictures confirmed this, including ones of them together, John perched on his Grandad's knee. Additionally, he'd seen shots of his grandparents' wedding, others of them larking around at the seaside, at the dog races, posing outside various places he didn't recognise and laughing inside the Richmond. Colour photos sat alongside black and white ones, but the evidence was consistent throughout. So too was the knowledge, John now realises, that he has seen the man opposite him before, or at least photographs of a younger version of the same person, for he undoubtedly featured in many of the pictures, standing there alongside his grandparents. John feels he ought to say something. He struggles though to find the right words, and so he utters the first thing that comes to mind: "I'm John. Alf was my Grandad."

Bert's jaw drops. His face is a contortion of incredulity. He initially feels relief – the stranger is not angry at him for having mistaken his identity. The next emotion is one of amazement: John, John... the name is certainly familiar, almost as recognisable as the features of the youth he beholds. It is all so hard for Bert; the past and present keep merging into one, everything getting terribly churned together and entangled. The cogs are turning furiously in Bert's mind, but they keep getting stuck.

The thing he had been trying to remember earlier, not that silly hallucination word, but what Alf and Jean's daughter had been called, appears. It is floating just in front of him and Bert grasps at it. That's right, it was Sylvie. She was a pretty little thing who'd fortunately inherited her Mum's looks and her Dad's charm. Bert and Iris would sometimes babysit her, a temporary substitute for the child they had never had. He recalls feeding Sylvie with fruit from his stall: "here, have another strawberry; they'll do you good love." They were a treat in those days, but how she adored them! Though that would have been ages ago; it must have been, if this is one of *her* children now facing him.

Bert thinks harder; it's an effort. Somewhere it's there, some story, lurking in the dusty chambers of his mind. It comes, eventually. He's pretty sure that he had heard Alf or Jean complaining about their grandchildren, or at least some of them. How many were there? He's not sure, but it doesn't matter. The problem, he recalls being told, was that they never visited (Sylvie rarely did either, although that was her Brummie husband's fault; Bert had listened to that lament many times), they never had any time for old people, were only interested in making money, jet-setting, buying flash cars and the like. But, if Alf and Jean were both dead, what could one of their no-good, disinterested grandkids possibly be doing in the pool's changing rooms? Had they even made the effort to come for Jean's wake?

"What are you doing here?" asks Bert, his voice containing surprise but resentment too.

John is taken aback by Bert's tone. He wonders what he has done this time, why the old man seems suddenly antagonised. The words come out improvised and unplanned, John wilting in the face of the challenge.

"Well. I've been swimming, but I didn't actually mean to. I wanted to use the gym, but really I came here in the first place 'cause I wanted to see…"

Bert's expression is one of increasing bewilderment and disorientation. Alf and Jean's boy is making absolutely no sense. The walls and the floor of the changing room begin to tilt again. Bert's hands are shaking, he feels dizzy and wonders if he is about to faint. Where is Iris when he needs her? Gone, to the same place as his friends. Bert's anguish is plain to see; evident to John, who realises that the old man is seeking comfort and reassurance, not confrontation and tension. What also strikes John is his foolishness. Bert, believing him to be Alf, had simply wanted to learn more about John, not what he might have been doing at the leisure centre. John wants to kick himself, and take back the words that have clearly caused so much additional confusion. Instead, he pauses, collects his thoughts, and then says very slowly, speaking in the voice he reserves for difficult customers when trying to get them to leave at closing time, "when my Gran – that's Jean – died, I moved into her flat. I've been there a little while now. I've got a job up the road, at Perfect Pizza."

"Perfect Pizza?!" Leon shouts the words with indignant urgency; Bert mumbles them bemusedly; and, from a distance, Archie repeats them, slowly and carefully. John is confused. He hasn't grasped the impact his words have had on the changing room, can't understand why everyone should be so interested in where he works. It's not as if it's a particularly exciting place, just a fast-food joint where he happened to land a job, somewhere he hadn't even set foot in a month ago.

Leon's morning has got progressively worse, a succession of hellish moments tumbling on top of each other. He has endured far more emotional turmoil in the minutes since his swim than he imagined possible. First, there was the man who called his son a silly kid; then there was the incident with the cleaner and the papers spilled on the floor, the confrontation with the lawyer that had followed, and his tears, their shared tragedy. Turning from Archie's collapsed form, Leon's priority had simply been to dress, leave the leisure centre as quickly as possible and find a nearby cafe where he could sit quietly until it was time for his shift. There, he would be able to think, process and analyse, then work out what he ought to do in order to attempt to get his life back on track and reconnect with the rest of his family.

However, in the few steps to his towel and locker beyond, Leon had spotted the young lad wearing a Perfect Pizza top. He was pretty sure he had never seen him before, but suddenly to be staring at the restaurant's logo, after everything else, had seemed like an affront, an unnecessarily cruel joke, reminding him once again of his loss. Of course, he knew the place, had been there a couple of times over the years (not that he rated it). But since Samuel's death, thoughts of it had plagued him constantly, for this was where his son was last seen, where he ate his final meal. Leon's thoughts are in a frenzy as he towers over John, wanting… in the heat of the moment, Leon is not sure… an outlet for his frustration, an explanation for why this boy might be at the leisure centre, answers to what Samuel might have been doing in his final moments – all this, and more.

John is sweating. Droplets of perspiration seep from his armpits, pooling unpleasantly in his tight jersey. Beads of moisture have formed on his forehead. His eyes are stinging again and he wants to cry. A visibly incensed naked man, far larger and stronger than him, is standing inches from his face, so close that John can feel his breath, hot and fast. John has always been a coward, the obvious target, too slow and lumbering to see the blow coming, the chair pulled away from him, the swinging door slammed in his face. There is nowhere to hide other than the possible refuge of the changing room floor, where he could curl, weak and defenceless, like the lawyer. The idea is quite appealing.

"Don't you touch Alf and Jean's boy!" roars Bert, raising his fists to Leon, heart hammering, yet feeling braver than he has done for a long time. Bert is transported back to his school days, the regular scuffles in the playground. He could hold his own and didn't like bullies. He would regularly look out for Alf; they would pick on him for being ginger, no good with his lessons, or at sports. The words Perfect Pizza have gone from his mind almost as quickly as they arrived; all Bert sees is a stranger menacing his mate's grandson, someone he was having a conversation with just a minute ago. Having not witnessed any of the morning's earlier curious events, he has no idea why this man should be so interested in John.

Leon's reaction is one of surprise. The fragility of the old man opposite him is evident, so much so that it looks to Leon as if he might keel over at any moment. He's seen him around at the pool quite a bit, was only thinking about him this morning before his swim. He had noted the man's decay and thought how his mostly cheery external demeanour must belie a deeper problem. Leon imagined they shared an unspoken bond, both seeming to adhere to a routine – the regular visits to the pool – since it represented some form of stability, one constant in a world where there seemed to be so few. Now, absurdly, not only is the man squaring up to him, but he appears also to know the ginger bloke with the Perfect Pizza top.

Before Leon can say or do anything (what, he is still not sure), however, he hears a rich and sonorous voice with which he is all too familiar pronouncing, "now gentlemen." Leon turns to see Archie standing beside him, towel now smartly tied around his waist again. John and Bert stare open-mouthed, uncomprehendingly. Archie feels restored; dare he say it, Promethean. Moments earlier, he had felt as if he might never emerge from the primeval anguish in which he was engulfed. It had overwhelmed him, taking him back to those tender and precious times with Herbie. All he could hear as he traversed the corridors of his past were the sounds of washing water, seemingly unending, until they were punctuated by the words "Perfect Pizza." They summoned him abruptly from his torpor, reminding him of his business for the day, that life had to carry on. He could not cry uselessly forever when there were things that needed doing and, of course, this was the place he was planning to visit later that day.

"What's all this about Perfect Pizza?" asks Archie.

"Well, I work there," says John (news to Archie, since it was only the final two words of the earlier exchange between John and Bert that had reached him).

Archie does not get a chance to ask another question, although his lips are already forming the words. Instead, Leon interrupts, almost pushing Archie to one side with his hand, the same one that only recently was placed consolingly on his shoulder. His quest is simply to know about Samuel, exactly what he may have been doing in his last minutes. It overpowers everything else, the lawyer's question delaying the answers he is desperately seeking.

"Were you working on the day my son got murdered?" The powerful insistence in Leon's voice is clear to John, but he is too scared to meet the man's glare. Instead, he looks down towards the ground, hoping it may swallow him up, or at least buy him some time before he has to respond. His eyes catch on the logo of his shirt and it now makes sense; that's why the man was staring at him. The realisation doesn't help though. John's tongue remains steadfastly tied, the words failing to form coherently. "I…," he begins.

It's all getting too much for Bert; it's a bit like that time he recently tried to go to the market on a Saturday, thought it would be fun to relive the old times, see a couple of his mates, have a bit of banter. He'd been looking forward to the event, but at the top of Church Street there were too many people, too much hustle and bustle; noise and shouting everywhere, voices other languages he didn't understand, not like it used to be at all. He had been forced to turn back. Bert feels similarly unsettled now, and wants desperately to sit down. He has been struggling to follow the conversation, the exchanges between the different people. It makes no sense to him why what feels like everyone in the changing room has gathered round him and John. And now someone's talking about a murder. Who just died? He doesn't remember hearing anything about it on the radio as he dressed this morning; and it didn't come up in conversation when he was having his roast with Ernie and Ned the other day, he's pretty sure.

"I don't understand," Bert says, "when was there a murder?"

Three voices respond simultaneously. Leon replies, "my son got stabbed just after he left Perfect Pizza;" Archie begins stentoriously, "on 18 April at 10…;" and John responds, "recently, it was the day when…"

Bert is more confused than before. His brow furrows and his wrinkles deepen. He forgets for a second where he is, unsure why there are three men standing so close to him, all speaking loudly and saying different things that make no sense. Why is one of them not wearing any clothes at all, while another has just a towel tied around his waist and a third seems to be wearing a shirt but no trousers? Bert's knees are shaking and he is shivering. He realises he is wearing only his swimming trunks. Was I just swimming, he wonders? Being in the water feels like a distant memory, perhaps from another day or a different era.

John feels sorry for Bert; after all, he was a friend of his Gran and Grandad, and now he looks so frail and defenceless, more likely to cry even than John. He wonders whether Bert has any grandchildren of his own, if they think about him with any regularity, and how sad it would be for him to die, alone, like his Gran. After all this is over, John wants to talk to Bert more, share a cuppa with him and hear his stories. He could do something useful for Bert and feel good about it. The novel thought occurs that Bert could become a friend, his first in London. For now, John simply steers him to the closest bench, sits him down and places his own towel (faded blue and white, with the Telford United logo incongruously emblazoned across its middle) around Bert's shoulders. Leon and Archie look on; watching, waiting until John has finished consoling Bert, Leon's earlier question still hanging unanswered.

Leon tries again, jabbing at John with his finger, his tone insistent, "were you working on the day my son got murdered?"

"Yes," answers John in a daze, still thinking about Bert and his own grandparents; how being old must be even harder than being young, Leon temporarily forgotten.

"And," Leon presses on, "what was he doing; what did you see?"

John pauses. He does not know what to say. He gave his statement to the police weeks ago and has nothing new or different to add, so he begins, his words reluctant and resigned: "well, he was there with some other boys, eating pizza and drinking coke. Actually, I think he ordered the chicken wings and chips." John sees that Leon is irritated by such details and so hurries on, wanting the ordeal to be over as soon as possible. It reminds him of being quizzed by the teacher in front of the class, something he never liked. He continues, the words now tumbling out quickly and spontaneously, with no thought given to their formation: "I then had to go to the loo 'cause my belly wasn't feeling right and… and then… when I came back, they were all gone."

A look somewhere between disgust and disappointment appears on Leon's face. It is replicated on Archie's. Leon has no interest in this boy's trip to the toilet, and the way in which he has described those crucial minutes of Samuel's life has rendered them profoundly mundane. He had been hoping for some recollection, preferably that Samuel was happy, had been laughing or was just living in the moment; not these banalities. Archie wonders from where this ginger twerp, whom he has never seen prior to today, may have emerged. He certainly wouldn't employ him, not even for a job in a pizza restaurant, let alone call upon him to appear as a witness in a court of law if he could possibly avoid it. John notices their expressions, and experiences once again that familiar sinking feeling, that he has done something wrong, spoken too much or not enough. He has no idea what to say now.

With all the attention focused on John, initially no one hears the low and faltering voice of Bert. He murmurs, as if in a trance, "I was there that night." Quick as a flash, Leon pivots to stare at Bert. Archie rapidly shifts position too. Mariusz remains frozen, fearful and hardly daring to breath in the room's corner. Bert continues, unaware of the altered atmosphere in the changing room, "I saw them all out on the street, I heard the police sirens."

Bert had begun to feel calmer, once seated and with the comfort of a warm towel around his shoulders. Those strange and slightly menacing people were still nearby, but they seemed to have forgotten about him and were instead talking with Alf and Jean's grandson for some reason. His heart had slowed and the conflicting thoughts that had earlier been crowding his head had become less frenzied. Yet the word murder still niggled in his mind, like a troublesome pain that refused to budge; had one happened recently, perhaps at the baths? Bert racked his brain. Fragments floated here and there; were they memories or just stories, maybe things he had seen on the TV? Throughout, however, there was one persistent image: a police board, as bright and yellow as the sun, blocking his way on the Edgware Road. Now, why was it there? That's right, there *was* a murder. There had been talk about it, Bert realises, even here in the pool's changing room not that long ago, and elsewhere too; he had heard his mates discussing it in the Richmond. The mist swirls, and then clears momentarily. The events of that fateful night come to Bert with sudden clarity. It was the evening when he had decided to go to the Lord High Admiral for a drink or two. He'd seen some youths as he walked back home, thought they were connected in some fashion with old Windrush Bob – so that's why he'd been on his mind earlier that morning – and then there'd been the flashing lights of the emergency services and their sirens. "I heard the sirens," Bert repeats.

Leon and Archie are now bearing down on Bert (John looks on, curious too), both thinking, albeit for very different reasons, now this *is* interesting, maybe crucial. The old man, they hope, may not be as feeble as he looks; rather, he could provide the key to the riddle, the vital evidence, or the answers to the questions that have been perplexing them. They are still processing the significance of Bert's revelation, so John seizes the opportunity and asks him, in what he hopes is a gentle and encouraging tone which may embolden Bert to speak further, "what did you see?"

"Yes, what did you see?" repeats Leon.

"Now exactly what did you see?" insists Archie.

The competing voices echo in Bert's ears, their faces crowd his. Everything is swimming in front of him. There are too many people present, not obviously connected, and what do they all want from him? Confusion reigns. Crazy and distorted pictures are swirling, twisting, turning, blurring and mixing before Bert's eyes. It's like someone has taken one of those toys he had when he was younger and shaken up its contents, a kaleido-thingie. The word eludes him, making him more troubled and upset than previously. Bert wishes once more that Iris were here; she would have the answers to all his problems, the forgotten words, the silly questions that everyone is asking him. Bert feels rushed, hassled, imposed upon. Where will it all end, he asks himself; was it always this complicated; why can't I just be swimming in a nice lake in Switzerland? Bert thinks he hears seagulls, but this can't be the case. He hears Iris telling him that "Switzerland doesn't have any coast, and it would be a long way for them to fly from the sea, silly!" The birds must therefore be here, crashing around in his head, fuzzing and blurring everything.

"Come on; what did you see?" There is impatient urgency in the tone. Bert has no idea who has said it; it doesn't matter, maybe he just imagined it. Why is this person, these people – he sees three unfamiliar faces staring at him – in such a rush; do they need to catch a bus or train; maybe a plane, to Switzerland? Things never used to happen this quickly, he's sure. Bert's brain struggles to get into gear. No, these people aren't travelling anywhere (quite the contrary); they are asking him a question. Now, what is it? That's right, it is about a murder; but whose murder, and why is he involved, was he there, did he witness it? Thoughts come and go, colliding violently and obstinately refusing to settle. Yet the expectant faces continue to loom ominously; thinking, waiting, hoping – that the moment when Bert remembers is going to come.

Part Three: End

MARIUSZ

And what of Mariusz? Everything now feels different. For him the leisure centre, or at least its changing room, has suddenly become a sinister place, populated by emotions and revelations, deep and unsettling. No longer is it simply somewhere to exercise and swim, where he can be one of many; another anonymous person amidst strangers, a small part of London's immense tapestry. Seemingly disparate lives and histories have been brought abruptly together, with terrible consequences. Mariusz has no wish to play any part in this at all.

Fresh out of the water, yet frozen like a statue by his locker (so close, yet unopened), Mariusz has watched the morning's events unfold: from the revelation that the man with whom he regularly shares a lane in the pool and sometimes chats about football was the father of the murdered child, through to the murmurings of the old guy, who said he had been on the street when the incident happened. It was unlike anything he had witnessed before, an engrossing yet obscene drama from which he could not draw away, but was instead impelled to watch with grim fascination. Throughout, there remained the constant reminder, a jarring loop, of his own stupidity; the inescapability of his involvement.

The misty and confused eyes of Bert settle momentarily on Mariusz. He is convinced that his guilt must be evident, can feel his face flushing brightly (even more so than the unfortunate cleaning attendant) and his heart thudding; the noise surely loud enough for all to hear, discordant amidst the eerie silence of the changing room. The unfocused gaze of Bert then drifts away again. But it rests on Mariusz for long enough for him to realise that he recognises that face and has seen it before, not just in the pool's changing room.

It comes to Mariusz, with harsh and brutal realisation, compounding his fears and worries. Of course, it was *that* night, the time he vowed never to deliver drugs for the Albanians again. He had been sickened by the whole experience, the nervousness of the boy, how young and innocent he looked, the incomparability of this youth's situation with that of his similarly aged brother, at home in Żary. Despite its forbidding exterior, the pub opposite the place he had just left, appeared as a beacon, a place of refuge. As Mariusz had entered, some of the locals had looked up from their drinks and stared insolently, sending a stark message that he was unwelcome. The expressions of the others despite registering his presence, had remained glazed. They were perhaps seeking greater inspiration from the dregs of their pints. The taste of his quickly-downed vodka returns suddenly to Mariusz's mouth, making him retch just as he did then, time looping back on itself. He brings his towel to his mouth, hoping that no one notices.

The faltering words, "I, I…" issue from the mouth of Bert. But then they stop as suddenly as they started. His hands are shaking, his lips twitching. Yet the faces of Leon, Archie and John lean closer, leering beseechingly, hungry like birds, hoping for more. No one can see the swirling seagulls within Bert's head, their flight relentless and unsettled. Another wave of acid rises in Mariusz's throat, and with it, the forceful awareness that he needs to do something; anything, other than remaining immobile, with only the shallow defence of his silence.

Mariusz looks longingly at the door of the changing room; the portal, the exit it provides to another world (the one through which Tony and the cleaner have already passed), the real world, of countless streets and multitudes of people. Here, he could lose himself easily. But, there is no way of getting to the door. Even if he could extricate his bag from his locker and dress soundlessly, his path to freedom is blocked by the circle of insistent figures surrounding Bert. To break it, Mariusz feels, would be tantamount to an admission or confession of his guilt; and he fears the clever words of the lawyer, the traps he might spring, as much as the dead boy's father's raw emotion. What to do? The sense of claustrophobia is tightening around Mariusz like a noose. Fretfully, he turns his head the other way and… there lies the swimming pool. It is so close Mariusz can feel it with all his senses: the profound blue, its murmuring waves, instantly recognisable smells and enveloping waters. All he wants is to be immersed, involved in a simple, repetitive and intuitive motion, putting space between himself and everything that has happened. There, he will be untouchable, in charge once again of his own destiny. He starts to move, swiftly yet silently. No one appears to have noticed. John, holding Bert's hand, is nervously tapping his foot, Archie is humming ever so quietly and Leon is pressing one fist restlessly into his other hand. Their eyes lie only on Bert. His quavering voice starts again, "I saw…"

Jedejn, dwa, trzy. Just three more steps to go, Mariusz calculates, and then he will be there, diving in, at the pool's deep end. He will be washed into its waters, carried away to somewhere distant, a new beginning, a rebirth in a different place. At this stage it doesn't matter whether it is in London or Żary; it could be Zanzibar for all Mariusz cares. This is an ending, one ending. The pool will still be here tomorrow, Mariusz knows, but he won't. He can never return. Its waters will continue moving unceasingly, but his secrets, like those of so many others, will remain, buried in its depths.

ISHMINA

What a very strange morning it has been and, it's not even eight o'clock yet. Quite a few things stand out, far more so than on a normal day here. Now let me see if I can get it all in the right order. Here goes. It began with a proposal. Almost the moment I sat down at the desk that terrible man – he calls himself Rodrigo from Rio – asked me if I wanted to join him for a drink that evening at the Green Man. As if! My rebuttal was met with a smirk as he headed off to the squash court with a chum of his.

I was still gathering my thoughts from this event as the usual stream of regulars entered through the doors: first came that pompous man Archie Knowles humming some ridiculous tune as ever, then the taciturn Pole Mariusz Jankowski, next Leon Campbell and, not long after that, poor old Bert Jackson tottered in. They're all here most mornings. I see many of them around the streets as well: Bert wandering forlornly, as if he were searching desperately for something he can no longer find; Archie in many of the local cafes and restaurants, Leon too. Archie is always by himself, but clearly on the lookout for people – anyone, seemingly – whom he can engage in conversation. He doesn't even live around here (this I know from my database). I am sure he must be running away from something. Leon Campbell also sits alone, but he is so different to Archie, always staring into space or with his head pressed into his hands as if he is trying to figure out the solution to some unsolvable problem.

During the flood of locals, I remember a guy entering whom I'd never seen before. He stuck in my mind, looking so out of place wearing a grubby top from Perfect Pizza. He had quite obviously never been to the leisure centre before and looked so disappointed, as if he were about to cry, when I told him that the air-conditioning in the gym had broken down. If I catch my brother Abdul before he heads back to university tonight, I'll have to ask him whether he knows the guy, whether they worked together. Even if he did eventually decide to use the pool, I somehow doubt I'll see him again.

Next, although I guess it must have been about half an hour later by this stage, came Tony Lecrowitz and his questions about the murder. And then, this is where it becomes curiouser and curiouser, Tony rushed out of the changing room and back into the reception area barely minutes after he had entered it. Clearly he hadn't been for a swim, so what could have prompted his abrupt change of mind? I don't think he even heard me asking whether everything was all right. All I recall is him pinching his nose and shaking his head as he departed in a rush, not even glancing back.

But – hold on! I've got things mixed up. Just before Tony made his hasty departure, that new cleaner – Ignacio, I believe, is his name – darted across the hallway in front of me. His mop and bucket were nowhere to be seen. Even without really knowing Spanish, it was obvious enough what he meant when I heard him exclaiming, far more loudly than is appropriate with customers around, "Madre del Dio! Basta!" – but I don't know why. Maybe I've been spending too much time thinking about them, but he certainly looked as if he had seen a ghost.

What could possibly have been going on in his head? And what might be going on in Mariusz's head? I'm sure it's his image I recognise in the corner of my flickering video screen returning to the pool – almost rushing – barely minutes after he just left it. I guess I'll never know. All I see is a small snapshot, a tiny fragment of these people's lives. The rest I'll have to make up, as ever. That's what I do while I sit here, for surely there is more than one side to every story: I invent histories.

Acknowledgements

While most of the locations cited in the novel exist in real life, others are fictional. The murder described fortunately never occurred and the characters are all a function of my imagination. Like Ishmina, my best source of inspiration for this work has come from living in and walking around the Edgware Road area for the last twenty years.

Nonetheless, I am hugely indebted to the help and advice provided by the following people, listed in alphabetical order to avoid any bias: Raficq Abdulla, Raf Aviles, Ray Barry, Adrian Beavis, Neil Cartwright, Mike Conaghan, Andrew Gunz, Barbara Gunz, Jonathan Gunz, Julie Gunz, Paul Hallam, Eleanor Hooker, Paul Lee, James Ross, Jennie Thorp, Nik Wilson.

20017376R00113

Printed in Great Britain
by Amazon